I0734728

Cindy M. Amos

SAVING BICYCLE MAN

by Cindy M. Amos

God flexes his mind—it's all-knowing,
He flexes His arm—it's all-powerful.
Tell me then, who can defy him?
He removes the mountains,
ere they are unaware.
Job 9:4-5

ISBN-13:978-1-944203-63-4

Dedicated to my devoted mother, Patsy P. Sawyer

The nurse who lovingly collected & put me back
together
after uncountable bicycle wrecks

The author would like to acknowledge the following
for their support and encouragement with this book:
Members of Jane's Gang book club from WEFC
Diana Grabau, Editor www.seizethedayedits.com
Janice Fairbairn, Marketing Strategist for LOM Series
Members of South Central Kansas ACFW Chapter
Cynthia Hickey of Forget Me Not Romances
& Inspiration of the Holy Spirit

LANDSCAPES OF MERCY SERIES BOOK TWO

Yet there is one ray of hope:
God's compassion never ends.
Only the Lord's mercies have kept us
from complete destruction.
Great is His faithfulness;
His lovingkindness renews each day.
Lamentations 3:21-23

Chapter 1

Cami Walsh chose to speed up Lookout Mountain again, a near-vertical landscape that had never been kind to her. Fresh off her shift at Golden's medical center, she could snag the snapshots she needed and still be home by the time her son's bus pulled into the complex. Though she felt optimistic about the plan, the mid-afternoon sun slipped further toward the western rim than she would have liked. She'd already wasted too many prayers wishing time would move backward so she could undo a few minor things, but eight years was long enough to realize that wasn't going to happen.

Bicyclists congregated at the base of Lookout Mountain, a popular circuit for local shift workers because the loop to the top and back could be tackled before dark. A gaggle of Lycra-wearing enthusiasts kneaded into a peddling mob as they flexed calf muscles and began their ascent, two by two. Once she'd maneuvered her compact car around the pack, she sped up so they wouldn't try to occupy the same space on the curvy narrow road. The bike path appeared an afterthought that reflected deep black asphalt, compared to the road's bleached gray surface. Her camera slid on the console, so she tucked it into the cup holder.

Why Mitchell had chosen Lost Beaver Trail as this week's science assignment she hadn't a clue. Oh, the trail drew enough interest as it rose at an angle on the mountain and entwined along the western face across two rockslides. He could have chosen more accessible places, like the nature trail along Clear Creek downtown. With the assignment due by week's end, she had not been successful diverting his attention away from the mountain, so here she was driving up to accomplish her motherly duty, as promised. A rap song started to play on the radio station, so she punched the select knob and brought up public radio's wordless tribute to the afternoon.

"Lord, I can only do midmountain today." She glared at the rocky vista ahead. "How about meeting me halfway?"

~

"Almost there." Holt Ellis checked behind him before the switchback ahead shortchanged his ability to see oncoming traffic. He downshifted for more traction, which allowed the bike to grip the road with a high level of capability. It had been a great metal steed and he felt a late-arriving swell of privilege to have owned it. A thought flitted through his mind that filming his ascent would have made a great marketing piece, but no one seemed interested in his commercial prowess as a marketing mastermind anymore.

The deep curve opened up in front of him as he approached the pinnacle. Today he would stop just short of the public parking area, out of fear that someone might recognize Bicycle Man from the recent newspaper feature. That didn't match his plan for the day, as his upcoming downhill mission necessitated a faceless victim of tragedy, and he didn't want to mix that desperation ending with his charitable success feeding the local homeless.   An exertion burn rose from deep within his thigh muscles, or what was left of them. His frame had atrophied after his unemployment benefits expired and left him short of ready cash. As much as he hated it, he had allowed himself to live off some of the donated food for the homeless that he delivered twice a week. Not among their ranks yet, he would have been if he'd chosen to stay and tough it out. His apartment lease expired in two days so he used that pivot point to set his "game over" plan into action. It represented the simplest way out by far.

Breathing fire on the final ascent, he gazed over the horizon, crumpled by the mountain. The valleys tucked between the ridges allowed for life in this hostile land. He had grown to love it, despite being a flatlander by birth. That origin had bequeathed him the ability to develop altitude sickness when he least desired it, although seven years had given him enough time to better acclimate to the thinner air. Bone-dry from the exertion, he took a pull from the water bladder latched to his back. He had allowed himself the luxury of water on this final ascent, one of the free blessings from God he had always appreciated.

Distracted by the high vista, he forgot to stop short

of the summit parking area until a catcall sounded from up ahead. A group of rowdy college kids roughhoused around a sleek convertible as they prepared to leave. Spotting a grove of Gambel oak near the roadside, he picked a stopping point and pedaled toward it. There he would wait them out so he could have the mountaintop to himself, one last time.

~

Cami scuffed her white nursing shoes on the curb, positioning to get a better picture of the trailhead signs for Lost Beaver Trail. She shot a couple of exposures and relaxed a little, turning a complete three-hundred-sixty degrees to see how the rest of civilization was enjoying the day. Intrepid mountains filled her view, with dots of hikers along the trail and a whir of descending cyclists. Deciding to capture the entire view, she set her camera on panoramic and faced away from the sun. Once the cyclists had gone around the turn, she snapped the shot sequence and turned the camera off to save the battery.

A young couple passed, arms tucked around each other. Cami motioned up the trail. "Have fun." The girl waved back as she stopped to tie her blond hair with a bandana that matched her boyfriend's. Cami tried not to let the scene jab her in the ribs, as love imbued the air in Colorado, only not for her. The couple stopped to study the trail map before heading out, which made her reflect how life would have been easier if it had come with a map, too. Maybe she'd be on course with her happily-ever-after if she hadn't gotten sidetracked during her nursing training. Still, she had the adoration of her son, and that would have to suffice for now, especially since she could deliver on the promised photos.

~

Holt realized as he sat on his bicycle that now there was only God—and him. That's what a mountaintop encounter should be like, right? Funny that for all the things he could have been feeling right now, gratitude surfaced and found expression first.

"Father, let me thank you for everything." His words drifted through the firs and oaks along the roadside. "I hope, in the end, you find me to have been a good steward of all you've entrusted to me. Please let somebody step in behind me with the food distribution and do a better job than I did so the homeless don't suffer further… Give my portion to someone who deserves it more, as lately I just feel like I've been taking up space. I know your mansion has many rooms waiting for your children, so when I get to the bottom of the mountain, I hope I'll look up and see mine. Thanks again for being mindful of my plight in your great compassion. You've always known what's best for me. Amen."

Head bowed, he made the conscious decision not to glance at the grandeur of the mountain one more time. He had allowed life to defeat him and now needed to focus on the downhill run. One sip of water launched him on his return trip. Between gravity, momentum, and a tailwind, surrender would be easier than he ever thought.

~

Plopping back into the driver's seat, Cami checked her hair in the rearview mirror. The image in the reflection caused her to sling the camera into the console and reposition her barrette to fight back her overgrown bangs. May had begun to sun bleach her hair full of highlights because of Mitchell's fondness for outdoor adventure. That equated to family time together, and with the shortness of summers in the Rockies, she couldn't begrudge him that privilege.

A gang of rowdy teens passed by in a convertible and her reverie shattered. A girl squealed in protest, followed by a roar of laughter from the guys around her. Cami couldn't stomach such immaturity. She had missed that carefree stage altogether. She'd barely completed nursing school when she gave birth to Mitchell. The boy's father had supported them only as far as the hospital, and then she'd been on her own with the baby.

Starting the car, she pulled the gearshift into reverse and pulled away from her assignment. She had six or seven shots for Mitchell and had let the saddleback winds scramble her hair long enough. With any luck, she would catch a tailwind on the descent and manage to beat the bus home. Pairs of pink-cheeked cyclists began trickling into the parking lot from below, and she braked to make sure they all arrived safely. A gang of four abreast came into the lot last, pulling up the rear in camaraderie. She steered the car wide to give them room to enter, then pulled out to go home.

~

The trip down to midmountain had been an exhilarating blur of movement. He had already become part of the bike now, emotionless and mechanical. Holt Ellis the man no longer existed. He leaned into the steady curve with precision and held it for three-quarters of a circle. The road planed out for the Lost Beaver trailhead and he decided not to brake through the straightaway. *On the final lap, you have to live life on the edge, a speed-driven fine line between balance and bedlam.* An olive flash glinted in the midday sun and the inevitable flanked him almost before he could react.

"Watch out!" His high-pitched voice sounded foreign to him. The car's driver veered, but not soon enough. His bike collided with the passenger side panel, and before he could leap away, his hip caught the side-view mirror in a clap of pain. In the sequence that followed, his bike wobbled and then disintegrated. His torso found the window where he face-planted and caught a glimpse of the mortified female driver. Falling away from the car, disappointment met with darkness, as he had not made the bottom of the hill.

~

"Lord, help me help him." Cami pulled off the shoulder of the road across the bike path. "I swear, I never saw him coming, Lord. Please let him be all right." Exiting the car, she stumbled off the road where the body of a man lay contorted into a fetal position, tangled in a cluster of mahogany bushes. Scrapes on his calves and knees bled as she knelt to check his vitals. When a moan escaped his throat, relief rolled off her shoulders, as she now knew he was alive—but not by how much.

"I'm a nurse, so let me help you." Cami pulled a branch off his neck to clear his face. Agony smeared his features and the stillness in his lower body didn't bode well. Wiping grit from his face, she leaned closer and blinked back tears as medical protocol came to mind. "I'll call 9-1-1 and get some help."

"No, no help." He flexed his jaw and clenched his

teeth. He lifted a gloved hand where the skin had been scraped off from his wrist to his elbow. "No money left, so no help."

He looked too thin on closer inspection, too gaunt even for a cyclist type. Golden had been hit pretty hard by the recession and left many without jobs, which made it hard to tough out the winters when the area's tourism slowed. His aversion to paying for professional help now stood as a blockade to her trained procedure to ask for it.

To gain clarity, she stood and braced against the back hatch of her car. Every ounce of her wanted to order that ambulance and get him the proper help. Guilt tried to blot out her rational thinking and she claimed a scriptural truth to knock it back. "I can't close my eyes to this, Lord. Please impress on me the right course of action. He's hurting and my carelessness put him there. Guide me through this decision. In Jesus' name, amen."

As she withdrew her hands from the car, a workable answer to the prayer settled on her. If he wouldn't go to the medical clinic, she'd have the clinic come to him. She would usher in his medical treatment, right from her own home. The Lord would have to guard her little family in the meantime. She drew a labored breath at the prospect of taking on the extra load as she unlatched the tailgate. The lifters guided it open and their smooth motion seemed to bolster her determination to get the repair job underway. "Let's get you into my car."

She tugged at his torso in an attempt to move him into a sitting position. Being upright didn't last for long. She wrapped her arms around his shoulders and lifted him to her side. He spat blood and had to rest the weight of his head on her shoulder to stay erect. In five dragging steps, they arrived at her car. Tucking his legs in after him, she closed the hatch door and started for the driver's side when the tangle of bike caught her attention. In a gut-wrench of obligation, she doubled back to retrieve what remained of the bike carcass, shoving it across the backseat.

The car ride down the mountain dripped with emotional pain as she considered how in the world she could provide medical help to this scraped-up, down-on-his-luck man. Of course, Mitchell would help her, as the boy had never met a stranger in his life. They would move the dining table over and set the houseplants out back on the patio, which would create a space right in the kitchen. There she would nurse him back to health while off duty and get him back on his feet again in no time. Problem solved.

A moan sounded from the back of the car as she waited for the traffic light at the foot of the mountain. Knowing how tight her budget had already been stretched, she could moan, too. She tapped the camera where it rested on the console and noticed a smear of blood on her hand. That struck her as some kind of symbol that they were both in this together now, for better or for worse. The light turned green and she prodded her little car toward home, down into the safe valley, far away from the brooding mountain.

Chapter 2

Through the windshield, the complex seemed comatose except for the school bus breathing life into the commons area. Cami gave the bus driver enough time to maneuver the turn-around and then pulled up to the parade of elementary school kids walking home.

She kept it light for the sake of the onlookers. "Hey, Mitch, want a lift?"

He wiggled from the pack and headed for her car, his freckled face animated at the special treatment. "You betcha." He shrugged the backpack off his shoulder to slide in, then sank into the front passenger seat and picked up the camera. "You got my pictures!" A moan echoed forward from the back of the car. The smile on his face deflated in an instant.

"I picked up a little bonus surprise along the way." She glanced in the rearview mirror, dropped the pretense, and deferred straight to deadpan. "Not a word until we get him inside, do you understand me, young man?"

The boy's mouth fell open as he turned and glimpsed the crumpled bike behind them. He nodded and slipped the camera into his backpack, as though to free his hands to launch into a secret mission.

"I can't do this without you, Mitchell. This man needs help and can't afford it, so we're going to doctor him." The driveway to their duplex opened off the front hood and she swung the car in with added haste. "Now help me get him inside. You can come back for your book bag." She exited while Mitch exploded out his door. When she lifted the back hatch, the bloody scene gave her an inkling of what she was up against. "Let's take him in through the patio door." She glanced around the side of the house for hazards. Granted, it proved longer than using the front door, but it spared the off-white living room carpet.

Each taking a side, they lifted the victim and managed to get him around the back side of the house. Cami flinched when the patio gate wouldn't budge, but Mitch dropped to all fours and scurried under the privacy fence. Sounds of the latch being jimmied soon followed and the gate swung open. Relief flooded over Cami as she realized she was raising a resourceful son. "Strong work." She gave him a moment to take his position opposite her. A struggle ensued, but they finally arrived at the back sliding doors, which she opened with a twist of her key.

"Put him right here beside the table for now." She pulled a seat cushion from a chair to pad the tile floor. Mitch mimicked her efforts, shoving his cushion under the man's shoulders. A calico cat tiptoed up to greet the family as she removed the victim's helmet. Despite scratches along his jawline and gaunt cheeks, his features struck her as ruggedly handsome.

The boy shooed the pet away. "Stay back, Scrubs. We're in triage right now."

Cami tried to laugh, but it came out more like a sob. She started to wipe her loose bangs away, but spotted the dried blood on the back of her hand and ran to the sink to clean up. Somewhere during her scrub down, the tears started flowing. As Mitch vanished into the front room, she wet a kitchen towel and stepped back into the dining nook to begin caregiving. Her patient had rolled onto his side, away from her.

"Let me start bringing you back to life." She let the unanswered tease drift past the wreckage scene. The patient shuddered under her touch, grunting. A fistful of roadside grit had embedded in the scraped skin along his entire left side. Even his stretchy biking shorts had ripped at the hip and now seeped blood. "Well, it looks like we're going to have to become more familiar on rather short notice." She tugged at his waistband to clean the wounds.

Mitch reappeared with two beach towels, the same ones they had been looking forward to using at the pool. Today, their function would be much more somber.

"Give us some privacy for a few minutes, honey. Could you clean up the car for me?" She tucked one towel behind the victim and he grasped the other one, tucking it to his front.

"Sure thing, Mom. Let me get my backpack in first."

"And throw that old vinyl tablecloth straight in the trashcan, being careful of all the blood." She looked at her son with pleading eyes. He smiled and turned on his heels to start the dirty work she'd assigned him. Looking down at the injured man, she saw that the tea towel had already saturated from a steady flow of blood from under the patient's left elbow. That would mark her starting point.

~

As much as he wanted to tell her not to bother, the incessant waves of pain made talking out of the question. Holt found the fortitude to hold his trunk rigid as his rescuer mopped across the length of his body in an attempt to stem the blood flow. Raw exposure to the air made it impossible for him to think. He became a skinless mass of connective tissue lying on a tile floor. The pain peaked to unbearable, and then came a blackout of peace.

Something acrid burned his nostrils, and the rescuer retracted a wad of cotton from under his nose, speaking in a soothing voice. He felt the delicate weight of a sheet being pulled up over his torso. With some struggle, he managed to open his eyes.

The woman lowered her face so he could see her. "I'm Cami. You're going to be all right. I'll make sure of it."

The wobble inside of him took over again and daylight dimmed around him. On the verge of weak surrender, he mustered his courage to form a coherent response. "Pretty lady," he uttered, his lips not quite meeting. And then the lights went out again.

~

Cami fumed into the phone. "No, you don't have a

choice, Bo. Well, my day has been more than a pistol, so don't even try to one-up me on that. Just bring the supplies I asked for and come right away." She punched the off button and exhaled her contempt, only to find her son looking at her in sympathy.

He sat behind the counter, mouth twitching from the tension in the room. His math homework strewn across the bar, the boy couldn't help but be distracted by their needy guest. "How about I make my killer tacos while we wait for him to show?"

Her mood softened, she placed her hands on his shoulders, rotating him on the stool. "What would I do without you?"

"Let's hope we never have to find out." He placed his chubby hand over hers.

"Water," croaked the patient from the mattress that now padded the floor.

"I'll get this." Mitch slid off the bar stool and stepped around the table. He slipped the siphon from the water bladder into the patient's mouth and let him become reacquainted with his own equipment.

A ripple floated down the length of the reservoir, a good sign that recovery had been launched. After all, without an IV, she couldn't force the fluid intake. He would have to do his part if he wanted to get back on his feet. Only Taco Tuesday, she had three more days of eight-hour shifts to complete this week. She would accept all the cooperation she could get. "Fine. You rule the kitchen then and I'll go start the laundry. Maybe some extra soap would be in order—and possibly a double wash for his things."

"How about a duct tape patch job after that?" Mitch yanked the refrigerator door open to get started on the only dinner he'd been taught how to make. "How'd the airplane glue work on his elbow?"

"Peachy keen. I fixed his wing flap and the blood flow stopped just like that."

"Good job, Mom. You're the best nurse ever." His thumb shot skyward to validate the boisterous claim.

She crinkled her nose at him and stepped back to the laundry room to get rid of the blood evidence, another sign of the return to normal she needed to happen.

~

Bo stepped through the doorway as though he'd grown allergic to the place. Dressed in creased khakis and a polo shirt, he looked prepped for anything but hands-on doctor duty. "This had better not be another stray cat. I can't bail you out every time you're feeling humanitarian, Camille. Stand up on your own two feet, for pity's sakes."

She dropped her gaze and motioned toward the kitchen. "I did all I could do, but his hip injury is causing me some concern. I needed a doctor to examine it more closely. Thanks for coming and bringing this stuff."

"Save your thanks and get ready for my flat refusal next time, as my spare time is precious to me. You have three minutes and then I'm on my way to something more attractive." He handed her a bag containing the medical supplies and stepped into the kitchen area. The boy stood with his back to him, rinsing dishes at the sink. "Hey there, Mitchell, old buddy, old pal."

Mitch wiped his hands dry. "Hey Bo, long time no see." He stepped down off a stool and came over to shake hands.

"So what kind of stray did your mom bring home this time?"

"Over here behind the table," Cami replied. She set the bag on the bar and led the way to the edge of the mattress.

Bo whistled as he caught an eyeful of scraped humanity hunched on the floor, asleep. "So, you finally got yourself a man? Had to run him over, did you?"

"Very funny, Bo. He ran into my car, cycling down Lookout Mountain. I offered to call for help, but he can't afford it. I think he's unemployed…"

"And therefore uninsured, which makes him a charity case that sucks my time off."

"Don't be so high and mighty. What about a little compassion for the less fortunate?"

"Oh, I have compassion aplenty. It doesn't curl up on the floor of my dining room and beg for healing, though."

"God says 'unto the least of these,'" Mitch said.

Convinced he wasn't going to win the battle, he knelt and examined the patient. Cami had mentioned the hip area seemed somewhat worrisome. Bo pulled the sheet down and flexed the man's leg carefully. The joint attachment proved solid. A gauze pad broke free with the motion and Cami's hands soon appeared next to his, adhering it back in place. The patient moaned, and he hesitated.

"I'll rule out dysplasia for now, and call it a contusion. That doesn't close the door for further complications, like a labral tear. But don't expect me to have x-ray vision. Any further setbacks have to be addressed at the clinic, is that clear?"

"Got it," Cami replied. "So his hip isn't dislocated,

which means Holt should regain use of his legs as the injury stabilizes."

Bo knit his brow contemplating the course of his recovery. "Let me come back in a couple of days when some of this has scabbed over. In the meantime, Cami, I see embedded gravel under his skin. You usually do better work than that. Try to have him cleaned up before my return."

"Bathroom," the patient moaned.

Bo laughed and a crooked smile unfolded, as the dependent cyclist might wish he wasn't so hobbled now that the urge to relieve his bladder pressed the issue. The boy scrambled to the kitchen cabinets and returned with an oversized melamine bowl with a cheery-faced cartoon character emblazoned on it to heighten the ridiculous scenario.

"Here you go, Live Strong." He passed the bowl to the wounded man. "It's time to visit Port-a-potty Squarepants, your new friend." The boy knelt closer to the scratched-up crash victim. Too bad compassion wasn't contagious. Impatient to end his charity work, he turned to leave.

Cami walked him to the front door. "Okay. We'll plan to see you on Thursday and I'll get the gravel out in the meantime. You brought the needle-nosed pliers, right?"

Bo nodded with a snicker. "I suppose it's a cheap thrill to touch a man without any skin."

"Ten times better than a man without a heart."

When she shoved the screen door open with her foot, freedom came by means of escape, his favorite methodology. Bo wiped his hands, trying to rid himself of any remnant of the unfortunate encounter. He had another tactic in mind for his return encounter, one that wouldn't be so sweet with cooperation. Cami didn't need another dependent, especially of the male variety.

~

The candle flickered between them and spread its warmth across the tiles where he lay recovering from an accident of intervention. Holt knew that God had stepped into his self-destructive plan, and now he felt the pain of being very much alive. Earlier, his hosts had spooned a dinner of strawberry smoothie into his mouth and, once again, circumstance forced him to accept the moment. Mother-and-son devotional sentiments drifted into his proximity where they hovered like a foggy layer of belief. One sentence about the impossibility of giving up struck a chord with him. When had he stopped feeling like that?

Cami smiled at him as she closed the book. "I'll be back after I tuck Mitch in." The candle shimmered in her eyes, and he saw an honest vulnerability there that touched him deeper than his pain-filled exterior. He nodded and closed his eyes.

"Don't forget I'm pulling for you," Mitch called from the doorway.

He managed to raise his right hand and signaled a weak thumbs-up to the boy as they left. It reminded him how many people had turned their backs on the unemployed and the homeless, the disenfranchised of earth. Only the watchful eyes of their heavenly Father caught them in a cradle of concern and, in his mercy, kept them. It seemed a meager hand-to-mouth life where the flicker of faith could barely hold its flame. Maybe that's how God wanted it.

Minutes passed before the dainty smell of

perfumed powder filled his senses and he knew she had returned. He opened his eyes and she appeared across the candle, lying on her stomach with her chin propped in her hands. This time he wouldn't allow himself to shut his eyes, and they regarded one another for what seemed to him like hours.

"Wonder what it is about you that God thought he had to bring to my attention in such a cataclysmic way?" She tilted her head to one side. Long bangs fell across her eyes and she left them there, like some statement of half-finished business.

"You're a nurse," he replied, his throat raspy.

She leaned across the flame, connected his siphon to his lips, and allowed him to draw liquid refreshment to squelch his parched existence. The action left her closer than ever, her gold-brown eyes reflecting him now instead of the flame.

Her compassion tangible, a pang of loneliness release inside of his chest that made him draw an uneven breath. "I need you." He rolled onto his back to give his hip some relief. Waiting for a response that didn't come, the candle flame gave out in a puff and nothing but darkness existed, tinged with powder. How long she sat there with him, he could only guess, but he did faintly remember the brushed-against sensation of being kissed goodnight as the moon showed itself high atop the patio door. Or had he dreamt it?

Chapter 3

“Goodness, sweetie, whatever happened to you?” Cami stared in disbelief at the young woman she had seen on Lost Beaver trailhead the day before. Stationed at the walk-in portion of the medical center today, she had seen a little of everything come through the door. Her shift now pushing eleven o’clock, she had contemplated more than once darting home to check on her cycling patient over her lunch break.

The young woman laid back on the examination table in surrender. “Well, for starters, never run down a mountain.” Her left ankle appeared swollen and stiff, but her right side held the majority of the bruising. Cami counted five areas of contact up her leg and hip, most likely from close encounters of a rock kind.

“So the left ankle gave out?”

“And my right side took the brunt of the fall—on

that first rock slide coming back down the trail."

"Ouch and double ouch." Cami sensed her misery. "Let me get your vitals and we'll have the doctor look at you. I think he's going to want to x-ray that left ankle, just to be sure it's only a sprain. Fortunately, x-rays don't land on you like rocks." She lifted the blood pressure cuff off its hook and encased the patient's thin arm with it, pumping it taut. Her tone softened as she pumped one last time. "I bet your boyfriend was beside himself with worry."

"Oh, he totally freaked out." She covered her eyes with her hand.

Silence lingered as Cami assessed the pressure reading and dutifully recorded it on the computer. Next she clipped a cap on the digital thermometer and placed it in the girl's ear as she hummed a comforting tune. Once she had that reading documented, she touched the patient's shoulder to get her attention.

"The doctor will be in shortly." Cami followed the promise with a slight smile. "If I don't see you after the x-ray, you take care of yourself—and see if that boyfriend is willing to do more than his share."

"Sounds like a real test of character."

"Yes, it does." Cami stepped away and pulled the door closed behind her. Placing the medical file into the door pocket, she glanced up the hall and caught Bo flirting with the new front desk recruit. Talk about predictable. The skinny blond laughed too loud and the sting of embarrassment trickled down Cami's neck at his unprofessional behavior. "Room three is waiting," she called down the hall, hoping to break up the all-too-public tryst. Bo threw a finger up to acknowledge her claim without the decency of honoring her with a look.

She turned her back and walked into the staff lounge. With a hand on her cell phone, she hit the first number on her favorites list and waited for the pick-up.

"I need a teeny-weeny favor today," she said, as anxiety tied a knot in her stomach. "And you won't have to go any further than next door."

~

The cartoon bowl mocked him, but Holt remained driven to get to a bathroom right away. He remembered hearing a flush on the opposite side of the bar, possibly near the laundry room Cami had busied herself in last night. Mitch had left his skateboard by the patio door, so he could sit on that and paddle across the tile floor like a land kayak. Stretching to the full extent of his length, his fingertips managed to connect with the sandpaper-like surface of the board. He pulled it back and got it wedged under his chest, an area tender from the window collision, but not scraped like his side.

Somehow his lower body didn't want to follow suit so he forced his hips over the last inch of skateboard. With one careful push backward, he cleared the bar separating the dining area from the kitchen. Now he could see his target just past the refrigerator, which gained him motivation anew. He navigated the makeshift gurney into a pivot and aimed for the kitchen island. As he passed the refrigerator, a familiar photo caught his eye. A mixture of intrigue and embarrassment swept over him. Cami must have clipped the feature article out of last week's paper. There he stood as Bicycle Man, delivering groceries to a homeless man.

Nature's call overruled his mental turbulence as he propelled himself toward the laundry room. He could see the toilet in the back corner of the room. Only one barrier stood between him and relief—a metal threshold. With all the energy he could muster, he shoved the skateboard forward, hit the threshold, and somehow launched airborne while his vehicle bucked and retreated the opposite direction. The sound of rolling wheels came to a sudden halt.

"Lord have mercy," a woman said. "What do we have here?"

"Must get to the bathroom," he replied once he'd regained the wind in his chest.

She set something down on the counter and approached him with a chuckle low in her throat. "I suppose necessity truly is the mother of invention." She cupped his shoulders in her sturdy arms and dragged him into the room, close enough his chin could have rested on the porcelain rim. "This good enough?"

"Fine." Humiliation from such a ludicrous first impression arose without expectation.

"I'll be waiting right outside the door, so give a shout when you're done."

"Much obliged, ma'am." The door latched closed. He stayed for what seemed like an eternity and occasionally heard noises from the active kitchen as the woman readied what he assumed to be lunch. Now he would be beholden to yet another gracious individual and couldn't seem to find a way out of the growing debt, given his condition. Seems he was much better at extending the hand of mercy than receiving it. *Well, nothing like a total wipeout to make a person learn something new about himself.* He swallowed his pride and made a loud knock on the door. It opened moments later and he saw a distinguished older woman positioning an office chair in front of him. Her eyes smiled from a relaxed face.

"I'm Cami's aunt, Joyce Lancaster. I live next door and occasionally get to be a guardian angel for my niece and grandnephew. Now listen. We're going to try something more substantial to float you back to bed, as the skateboard isn't my speed and apparently not yours either. I want to lift you into the chair and see if you can navigate it while I set out your lunch."

"Yes, ma'am. At this point, I'm game to try anything that gets me back on the road to recovery."

"I like cooperation in a man." She seemed amused, stirring something in her bowl. "I'm sure Cami appreciates it, too. She has her hands full enough raising Mitchell by herself." She approached and bent to lift him.

Holt clenched his teeth to offset the pain of contact flexing his scab-covered skin. The seat of the chair made for a short trip, though. He instantly enjoyed the position of sitting, as long as he kept his weight shifted off his injured left hip. "Maybe I could pull over to the bar and eat upright like a paying customer."

Joyce cocked a well-manicured brow at him and swung a bamboo tray around. It plopped onto the end of the bar. Her hands now free, she launched him up beside the overhanging rim. A lunch of tuna and crackers, cheese, and apple slices waited for him. "God, we thank you for this day, this companionship and this food," she said without warning. "Please help this young man get better. Amen."

"Amen." Holt opened his eyes and fazed back into humanity. The food actually smelled appetizing and his stomach growled in response. He scooped a cracker through the mound of tuna and drew it toward his mouth.

"If I'm going to pray for you, I'd prefer to know what to call you. Let's be traditional. What did your mother name you?"

A smile tucked into his scratched cheeks. "Holt." Her maternal tendencies won him over and he began to relax in her company. The tuna landed in a delectable first bite. Another part of him came alive again. How great to have made a new friend to help usher it in.

~

Late for lunch break, Cami looked out across the waiting room and puffed through her bangs. The morning's rush had subsided. She flashed a signal to the medical clerk and turned to head for the staff lounge to retrieve her sack lunch. Suddenly, a patient bolted from the examination room, hobbled by injury yet visibly desperate to exit. Cami lost her next breath, as she recognized the young mountain climber. When she got a good look at the woman's face, tears intermixed with unvarnished fear.

"Try to stay off that ankle this week," Cami called behind her. A slight wave acknowledged her concern. When she turned to face the room, Bo stepped out with a sheepish look on his face that cooled to feigned authority. A rock landed in the pit of her stomach and lunch soon became a moot point. The travesty had played itself out again in an encore of seedy misbehavior. The sudden urge to heave wracked her frame.

Chapter 4

Cami shook the chicken thighs inside the bread bag, coating them evenly with her favorite mix of flour and spices. Her mind reflected on the new information her aunt had given her about their in-house patient. Aunt Joyce had enjoyed more success getting name, rank and serial number from him than she had been. Mitchell slammed his pencil on the counter behind her and gave a heavy sigh.

"Has anyone ever been killed by Social Studies?" he asked, making his fourth grade difficulties seem melodramatic. Their houseguest snickered as she placed four pieces of chicken into the frying pan. This new subject managed to come up with frequency during their nightly routine of dinner prep with homework, so she made an effort to keep him moving forward.

"What's the assignment, honey?"

"We're in a unit called economics," he replied with

a groan. "My worksheet is called 'Marketing Made Easy,' only it's not easy for me."

Cami turned the faucet on and washed the excess coating from her fingertips. She heard the office chair's wheels squeak and thought their patient might be showing some interest.

Holt pointed at the paper as he sat askew in the chair. "Read me something off your list."

"Write a slogan for each of the following products to launch a successful ad campaign," the boy read out with no inflection whatsoever.

Cami stifled a laugh and glanced at the two of them across the bar. She caught Holt's gaze and noticed a twinkle in his eyes for the first time.

"First entry, please," Holt said. "Pick one you like…"

"Mom always makes me go in order, so I don't leave something out."

He dipped his shoulder at the boy. "Well, tonight a new homework coach is in town." Cami nodded her approval as she walked by to check her supply of frozen veggies.

Mitch waggled the pencil in his fingers. "Okay. How about we try Dr. Pepper?"

"Now first, you have to think about what the product is, then you try to link it with how it makes you feel." Holt braced his left elbow onto the bar, grimaced and exchanged it for his right one.

Cami passed by with a poly bag of green peas. She found the exchange intriguing.

"Well, Dr. Pepper is a soda, so I drink it," the boy replied. "And it makes me feel…like a burp-meister, mostly."

"Make an attempt, Mitchell." Cami knit her brow to enforce the request and tried to ignore the laughter behind her.

"Think of something that means the same thing as a drink—like liquid," Holt said. "Then link it with something more hip, like an attitude you get from drinking that brand."

"You mean like an edge?"

"Perfect pitch, Mitch." Holt offered immediate reward for the answer. "Now put it together and you have your sales slogan."

"Liquid edge," the boy recited as he wrote down the entry. "That's smooth. I like it. Next entry is Dog Chow. Maybe I could use a nickname for dogs, you know, like 'man's best friend.'"

Cami turned from sink as she sensed that Mitch was not only teachable, but might be a quick study on top of that. Holt must have read her expression because he gave a little hidden wink that snagged her heartbeat and set a sensation loose that she couldn't identify. The two feelings intermixed, as she now had help with her son and she sensed an emotional awakening from a long, dreamless sleep.

"Maybe man's best friend gets his value by what he's fed," Holt suggested.

"Sorry it's only chicken thighs for us tonight," Cami replied, as the dog food suggestion seemed like a commentary on the quality end of dinner. Silence followed her comment until the chair wheels squeaked. When she looked up, Holt stared at her across the bar.

Something akin to hunger washed his face with honesty. "Before today, I hadn't eaten any meat for a month," he whispered. His gray-blue eyes softened, not with pathetic self-pity but with something deeper, more moving.

Cami turned away and busied herself flipping the chicken. Quality was subjective. She would be honored to serve chicken thighs tonight and they would eat together like royalty.

~

Holt remained at the island bar after dinner to maintain contact with his host family. His immediate hunger now satisfied, he allowed the low-key evening routine to lay comfort over his exposed skin patches.

Mitch glanced up from the front page of the weekly newspaper. "I can't believe it. Now Bicycle Man is missing. It says he never made his pickups this week. The store manager at Save Always claims that the overripe produce and expired bakery products are piling up because no one showed up to distribute them to the homeless this week. Mom, how can we let that happen?"

Holt sensed the boy's concern over the injustice of the situation but tried to hide the shame that swirled inside his chest. He crossed his ankles as if to brace for more.

"What can you do, Mitchell? You're only in fourth grade and you don't even have a bicycle to make the deliveries." Cami faced the boy, her mouth twisted to one side.

Heat registered under Holt's shirt collar and began to radiate up his neck. His negligence now festered as a new problem for his well-meaning hostess and he sat helpless to stop it. "Um, maybe you should pray about it first." Holt recognized that might buy them some time.

Cami tossed him a nod as she stepped over to put her arm around the boy. "Honey, I think Holt is right. We should ask God first and then be ready if it feels like the right thing to do. Besides, Bicycle Man is probably just out of town and forgot to let them know."

Dissatisfied, the boy tore away from his mother and disappeared into the hallway. His room door slammed to punctuate his objection to waiting.

Holt stiffened in the chair and lowered himself onto his makeshift bed to ease the ache across his pelvis, a move of surrender. He glanced up at Cami who stood nearby, staring out of the patio sliding door. A thought came to him that was so out-of-the-question, he knew it could only be the Spirit's beckoning.

"I have a bike, my boyhood bike, back at the apartment. My lease is up tomorrow and they'll be throwing my stuff out if I can't get back over there to claim it. What do you think about rescuing it for Mitch?" He waited, eyes closed, to allow her to process his invitation. Before he knew it, she sat down on the floor beside him, her face hovering inches above his. This time, he took an unhurried inspection of her features. He drank them in like a man who had just crossed the desert.

"Who are you, Holt Ellis?" Her words floated down and covered him with intensity. "And can you tell me why nothing feels the same since you came down that mountain?"

His throat parched dry, he could only glance up at her, but hoped his earnestness somehow showed. A fingertip touched his stubble-covered chin, birthing an ache deep inside, unconnected to his skin, a totally separate realm.

~

Cami lifted the bike from the hatchback and watched Mitch weld himself to it with purpose anew. He tore down the driveway toward the community center to test out every part of the pedaled vehicle. The sound of water spraying came across the front of the duplex as a familiar figure appeared. "Hello, Aunt Joyce." Cami stepped closer, trying to spot Mitch down by the playground. She picked a few shriveled leaves off the rose bush by the living room window.

"Haven't seen you out much, Cami. How's your houseguest?"

"So much better, it's startling. Thanks for covering for me at lunch today."

"Consider it my pleasure," Joyce replied. "Despite the scrapes and bruises, he's pretty easy on the eyes. I can do it again tomorrow if you'd like, but I have bridge club on Friday."

"That would be great for tomorrow. I asked for Friday off so I can be home with him."

"Have you thought much about after that?" She directed the water stream across the yet-to-bloom flowerbed. "I don't have anyone lined up for house-sitting my place when I take off Memorial weekend. That would keep him close by—only if you wanted that, of course."

"I'm afraid I don't know what I want." Cami craned her neck to see where the bike rider had gone. "I know his apartment lease runs out tomorrow, as I just rescued several boxes of his stuff when I picked up the bike for Mitch."

"Why don't you simply ask him and see if he's interested in the place? That would give him the honor of having his own space but put him close enough that you could keep tabs, especially until he didn't need any medical help." Joyce hummed as she watered another dry spot in the lawn.

"Then what?" She stepped toward the curb like her answer would come rolled up and tied with a rubber band, like the newspaper.

"You follow your heart. That's what."

Mitch reappeared and pedaled home, alternately holding the handlebars with one hand and then the other. Aware that their houseguest brought new territory for her family, Cami assessed the risk, like riding with only one hand on the wheel. Mitch glided up the driveway with a Grand Canyon smile and her worries shattered as if make-believe.

~

The devotion had been more optimistic tonight, Holt reflected, watching the candle burn down inside the jar. Earlier he had sketched a simplified route from Save Always store to the main homeless locations on the back of his dinner napkin. He planned to give it to Cami after she put the boy to bed. His strength improving with a better meal plan over the last few days, he propped up on his good elbow until she came back, wearing baggy PJs and smelling like sweet powder. When she sat, he slid the napkin note toward her over the tiles and gave her an encouraging look.

She held her peace for several seconds. "Something happened at the clinic today, something that I don't think is right. I made a passing acquaintance at Lost Beaver Trail—right before I made friends with you."

"Hope that came off a little softer than our run-in."

Cami's mouth tugged into an exaggerated grimace. "A young couple heading up the trail paused long enough for her to tie on a bandana that matched his. I remember thinking how quaint that gesture seemed, just a little thing, and told them to have fun. Anyway, she must have had a pretty bad fall later on the trail, because she came in today all banged up with a sprained ankle and rock bruises down the opposite side."

He touched his thumb to her knuckles to show support. "You probably get a lot of that, right?"

"Sure. But what I don't get is crippled patients running out of the building in tears after they've seen the doctor." Cami drew a labored breath before continuing. "A few seconds later, Bo let himself out of the exam room with a sly smirk on his face, like I haven't seen that expression before. Then he went right back to flirting with the new front desk receptionist. His behavior is out of control and no one appears to be willing to stop him."

"One day someone will." He crossed his arms over his stomach and released himself to a wave of weariness. A puff blotted the candle out and she nestled against the far edge of his pillow, humming. All tension seemed to leave the room and only pleasantness remained. This time when he sensed her cheek-brushing goodnight gesture coming in the dark, he rallied enough to greet it with his own sentiment. The skin pain vanished as the night dissolved to sweet powder all around.

Chapter 5

Geriatric patients offered Cami so much consolation she considered whether she should ask for permanent assignment with them. Her latest patient had taken a nasty fall, with a split forehead to accompany his broken hip. Head wounds always looked worse than they were. Even so, she swabbed an alcohol wipe below the stitches with extra care. When he winced, she stopped.

"Accidents happen and somebody always has to pay," the man said in a flat tone.

"Well, if it hadn't been for your accident, I never would have had the privilege of meeting you." Cami smiled as he reopened his eyes. As she shoved the tray away from the bedside, her focus flitted to her other patient, the one at home, occupying her every thought.

The patient chuckled. "Say, you seem to have a faraway look in your eyes. Could it be you might be working on an accident of the personal type, too?" He cocked a crooked finger toward his heart.

She nodded and pulled the privacy curtain across the semi-private room. Peeking back in, she pointed to her temple and poked herself.

"My trouble is the mismatch between here," she admitted, "and here." She lowered the accusatory finger to her chest and tapped as if to check for hollowness inside. "Try to rest quietly and let the healing begin." As she turned back toward the nursing station, Bo headed her way. She held her shoulders high to brace for the volley.

"Hope you're still expecting me this afternoon." Bo's tone seemed as fake as his smile.

"Only to check the left hip function, nothing more." She glanced at the chart in her hands.

"Oh, about that crying young woman yesterday. I guess she had an aversion to the x-ray results." He shrugged his shoulders.

"Can't say as I blame her then." Cami stepped away. She needed to put space between them. Fortunately her uniform hid the shudder quaking down her back. Halted in front of the desk, she made a promise to herself while the encounter remained fresh in her mind. She would not cover up for Bo from here on out, not an ounce.

"Mr. Carmichael in 201 needs assistance," the phlebotomist said. Cami pumped a dollop of hand sanitizer onto her palm and worked it in on her way to help another hurting soul.

~

Holt stared at a fancy tray of delectable food. "I certainly don't deserve this." While Joyce busied herself with his drink by the sink, he noticed she seemed too dressed up to be knocking around the house. "Are you going out today? You look spit-shined for something."

"Ah, young man, you have a keen eye for detail." She placed a sparkling glass of juice in front of him from across the bar. "I'm leaving town soon, so I'll begin my farewell rounds today. I leave Colorado every summer and go back east to spend time on the rocky shorelines of Maine, somewhat like a snowbird migrates, but exactly perpendicular."

"It seems to suit you though, so who's to say what the right direction is?" He picked up the glass to take a sip.

"Which brings me to my proposition for you, if you are well enough to consider it." She looked at his left arm and nodded with approval

"Continue on, Sideways Snowbird." He shoveled a bit of cream cheese spread onto his round cracker. The salty garlic mix awakened his taste buds and he enjoyed the satisfaction of culinary recovery.

"I always try to find someone trustworthy to house-sit for me the three months I'm away. You know, someone at church might have a college-aged offspring returning to town or something of that nature. Cami could keep an eye out for mischief around the duplex, but I prefer having someone live there. It gives me the opportunity to bless someone and feel like my investment is being taken care of at the same time. Does that make any sense to you at all?"

"Why, yes ma'am, it does." Holt took a spoonful of macaroni salad next. It possessed the perfect balance of creaminess and good taste. When he reached for another spoonful right away, she smiled. After clearing his mouth, he set the spoon down. "I'm afraid I couldn't pay you for the pleasure of staying next door, as much as I might want to." A dull ache slid through his heart as he realized that, once again, his existence came down to a lack of funds.

She dabbed the lipstick in the corner of her mouth. "Did I infer there was a cost? How detestable of me if I did. No, this is a free blessing, to help someone who may otherwise be falling through a crack. It's my version of searching out the lost coin from the Bible, as I rejoice that I can stand in the gap for someone…in transition."

He hung his head in humility, catching a glimpse of the goodness in her intent, a reflection of a giving heart. Something shifted inside, like a collective will to move forward. He'd forgotten what traction felt like. He looked up at her in gratitude. "Can I simply say I'll take it, or would you like me to sign something?"

"How positively wonderful." She smiled, and all her wrinkles disappeared in a countenance of grace. "No need to sign anything legal and binding. Just be reasonable with the power consumption and respect my things. That's all I ask. Cami has my phone number if anything breaks down and needs repair, so you can channel any such type of request through her. And I'll be staying in touch throughout the summer. I promised my dear sister I would."

"I'm a one-light-bulb-on kind of guy, so you don't have to worry about my energy consumption." He reclaimed the spoon. A chunky salad emerged as his next target, and the ranch dressing sat on it like a halo. A thought came to him that needed some closure, so he decided to test his source to see what kind of information he might be able to gain.

"What should I know about Cami?" His expression reflected his interest, with the hope he wasn't being too forward.

Joyce turned back to the sink. The water ran as she rinsed a plastic lid and placed it in the drainer. "I can tell you she's poured her whole life into Mitchell, and that she's a devoted mother." She spoke with her back turned. "Ever since nursing school, she's had to balance both child and career. She's done an admirable job and I'm proud of her." She sniffed into a tissue.

He realized that he had pricked her heart, which hadn't been his intention. Still, he pressed for the truth. "What happened in nursing school? I mean, did she have a boyfriend that wouldn't man up to being Mitch's father?"

"No boyfriend, no dating, not even a steady male friend." The woman turned and tried to control her facial contortions as strong emotions surfaced. "Which doesn't make sense at all, I know, given the outcome. But Cami sealed up tighter than a drum about whatever happened and I've never been able to get at the heart of the matter."

A growing awareness started in his lower gut and became a suspicion by the time it seeped into his brain. He wouldn't venture any accusations yet, but his hunch required some examination. He pretended interest in the food scraps left on his plate. "Cami seems the most giving person I've ever met. I would never do anything dishonorable to complicate her life, I can promise you that."

"You don't have to say anything, young man, as

it's written all over you, under the scratches that is. And scrapes and scratches go away, which leaves a man with an open heart who has to decide what he wants in life." She cleared her throat and her expression lightened. "Now that you have your things, what say we get you a shower today? After all, the doctor is coming this afternoon and we want to be respectable, don't we?"

His involuntary laughter sent the last mouthful of salad spraying across the counter. There was no way he could pretend to be respectable, unless scabs held nobility.

~

Mitch banged through the front door as Cami settled a headband over her bangs. "Holt! Holt! I've got big news!"

"Slow down, buster." Cami helped him slide the backpack off his shoulder.

He stooped to fish out several papers and shoved one at her as he literally skipped into the dining area.

When Holt tried to wake up enough to match the boy's enthusiasm, she found it comical for some reason. She leaned on the doorway, watching them interact.

"First, I got the best grade in class on the Social Studies assignment," Mitch said.

Cami found and held the paper up to show off the large A+ written in red ink at the top.

Holt raised his right hand and took the boy's high five as they celebrated the joint effort.

"For my reward, I'm the only one in fourth grade that's being allowed to compete in the upcoming Save Always slogan competition. The winner gets free groceries for a month. Man, oh man, think how many homeless people we could feed with that!" Mitch started an exuberant little anticipation dance as Holt clapped along.

Cami laughed and wiped a tear away at the same time. She rested her gaze on Holt, admiring his cleaned-up appearance and his ease with her son.

Holt rubbed his hands together like he couldn't wait to get started. "Tell me what Save Always wants and we'll start brainstorming the ad slogan together. It has to be a real winner, yet sincere at the same time."

Cami crossed the room and tacked the sheet onto the refrigerator door, moving the Bicycle Man feature over a smidge to share the magnet. The man in the picture looked a little familiar, but she couldn't quite place him. Today Mitch started his hunger relief bike route, so Bicycle Man could just stay missing.

"In fifteen words or less, tell how our store has made an impact in Golden," Mitch read from the contest flyer. "Make us proud of our heritage in the grocery business and we will use your slogan for our marketing campaign for the coming year. Does that sound great or what?"

Holt nodded at the boy. "Truly great." He pushed the napkin with a sketch on it toward the boy. "First things first, I guess. We've got to get you going for your debut as Junior Bicycle Man, so you need to understand this map."

"Okay, Holt. I'm ready." The boy handed the contest flyer to his mother and moved closer.

"Of course you'll start the loop at Save Always." Holt tapped at a star. "Go back to the produce department and ask for Bruce. He'll bring out the overripe fruit and vegetables in bags, so go get that loaded onto the bike. Then come back and get baked goods from Miss Julie. Got it?"

Cami couldn't shake the ill at ease feeling scratching the back of her throat. Mitch had never tried to carry so much responsibility before. "How about I go with him this first time, at least to the store?"

Holt looked up. They exchanged weighted glances and he nodded.

Relief swept over her as she tucked her overgrown bangs behind her ear. "Sure, I can help you balance the load, plus I'd get to meet the people who make this delivery possible."

"Okay, Mom," Mitch replied. "But this is really my thing, as I'm the one feeling God calling me to do it."

Holt tapped his finger on the first X marked on the loop.

Cami bent over his shoulder to take a look at the details. His face smelled like soap, which made her move closer.

"The first stop is under the Main Street Bridge where the homeless live." Holt traced his finger over the drawn arch. "There's a flat rock on the east bank that juts out into the creek. Stand there with the bags in your hands and your customers will come to you."

"How will they know to trust me?" Mitch shrugged his shoulders. His expression seemed pained that he might lack credibility with these strangers.

Cami turned in anticipation of Holt's answer and realized she was way too close. A magnetic smile deflected her way and suddenly she was caught in a trap of her own design, mesmerized by proximity and fully unable to escape.

"You have to let them trust you by acting

trustworthy," he replied. "Always look them in the eyes and let them see the love of Christ. He's your reputation." Holt turned from Mitch to her as if to solidify the point.

"This is a big risk," Cami added, unsure of which part of the plan she was talking about. Her focused intentions began to come unglued. She swallowed to ease her apprehensions. Maybe she would have to follow Mitch around the entire loop his first pass to make sure everything transpired peaceably.

"Remember, love covers a multitude of sins." Holt slid his finger to the next spot, also on the creek. "Stop in the trailer park above Clear Creek next. Do you know where that is?"

Cami focused even harder now, though her pulse pounded with a roar. Holt had spoken of love without realizing the effect his words had on her. How long would she be able to cover that up?

"Yeah, I know it. That's where I put in my inner tube up by the water park when I float the creek."

When Holt rewarded him with another broad smile, Cami had to stand straight up for a moment and remove herself from the zone of vulnerability.

"Okay, then. Hang around ten minutes or so to let the word get out that you're there. When the people stop coming, you'll know it's time to move on."

Alarm bells went off in her head that he seemed to know so much detail. She dug her nails into her forearm until it hurt. "How many more stops after that, Holt? I'm getting a little uneasy about some of this."

"Only three more, and they go really quick." He traced the loop closed with his finger. "These are all loading docks at three adjoining businesses. There, you divide what's left and leave the food on the top steps of the loading docks. There's no need to hang around."

"Great, that's a relief." She stepped into the kitchen to break the huddle. "Because I feel the need to shadow Mitch, I'll call Aunt Joyce and see if she can come over and supervise your doctor visit, as Bo still plans to come by this afternoon."

Holt shoved back from the counter. "I can handle Bo one-on-one. Besides, Aunt Joyce is making her farewell rounds this afternoon. She may not be back yet."

"Then I'll just leave a message." Cami hid the concern tightening her face with the cell phone as she crossed the room.

When Holt threw his hands up in surrender, Mitch laughed. "I just give in, too," the boy admitted. "It makes it easier in the long run."

"I heard that." Cami stepped into the hallway toward privacy. She slammed the door and dropped back onto her bed to calm her emotional state of imbalance. "Aunt Joyce, if you're home later, could you pop in and check on Holt for me? Bo plans to drop by and assess Holt's progress with his hip injury. Thanks a million. Let's catch up later. Love you. Bye-bye." She heard Mitch rustling through his closet through the wall adjoining hers, and in a matter of seconds, he appeared at her door with his "I love Jesus" T-shirt on. She had to chuckle at his obvious attempt to appear trustworthy.

"Let's roll, Mom." The boy slapped his hands on his sides.

She stood to honor his request. "Go get the bike and I'll load it in my car. I need to say goodbye to Holt on my way out." She soon heard the sliding glass door open and shut which cued her to make an appearance in the dining area. When she stepped into the room, Holt was watching the boy maneuver the bike out the gate. She cleared her throat. He turned toward her with the most remarkable look of satisfaction on his face.

"You and I need to talk when I get back home," she said, as devoid of emotion as she could manage. "Keep an eye out for the doctor, as he will likely arrive before I get back."

"No worries, Cami. I've got this." He cradled his chin with his good hand and nodded.

She squeezed her eyes shut to block out the sentiment and turned for the front door. The hasty exit struck her as fleeing, ironic because this was *her* home. Maybe what she needed to run from was on the inside, impossible to escape. Another type of collision loomed, a head-on collision with her suppressed emotions. Once safely outside, she shouted a protest that echoed clear to the mountain range on the edge of town. Only this time, it wasn't the mountain that hemmed her in.

Chapter 6

Holt flinched as someone slammed the front door latch, which put him on full alert. A tall figure appeared centered in the dining area's arch, and he recognized the doctor who had hovered over him on his first day here.

The man looked down the hall and regarded the almost empty house before walking into the room.

"What—no Cami?" He plopped a bag of gummy candy on the counter.

"No, she and Mitch are on a mission right now," Holt replied, not intending to add details. "You must be Bo. I'm afraid I don't remember much from the other day."

"Yeah, you're looking much better." Bo gave him the once-over. "Must be all that TLC that Cami tends to show the banged-up strays she drags home."

Holt maintained the higher road. "I'll be the first one to admit that she's been remarkable. It was a wipeout not to be repeated."

"Tell me how your accident happened." Bo leaned on the table, his tone insistent.

Holt knew how to handle Bo's type, though his smugness was reprehensible. "I got careless coming down Lookout Mountain on my bike and met up with her fender at the parking lot for Lost Beaver Trail. In her defense, she tried to swerve, but I had descended at a daredevil pace and there wasn't much either of us could do to avoid the collision."

"Well, I'm glad you're on the upswing, because vehicular manslaughter would lock Cami away, and the boy wouldn't have anyone to care for him." Bo patted the bag of candy.

"Oh, she's dragging around some guilt over her part, but I've been working on that."

"I bet you have." Bo gave a cheap grin and mocked him by rolling his eyes.

Holt studied the man's features a moment and something struck him as somewhat familiar. Little things, like the way his earlobes attached and the dip of his hairline. In an instant, it came to him where he had seen those features before—on Mitch. Suddenly he wanted to retch, and then an unexpected anger started to burn down low. He strategized to shift the focus. "I appreciate you stopping by, as it still hurts to stand. My left hip doesn't seem to want to bear any weight yet." Holt indicated the area of concern with a sweep of his hand. "Tell me, have you and Cami been friends a long time?"

"Long enough for me to be a little protective." Bo shrugged and pointed over his shoulder. "Listen, I need to take a glimpse at that hip again but a reclining position would be best."

Holt nodded and slid out of the chair to a position of relinquishment as lowly patient. He needed this expert medical treatment but it goaded him to no end that he had to take it from the likes of this self-absorbed specimen.

Bo knelt on the mattress. "Now roll over on your right side for me."

Holt hiked his shirttail up and rolled onto his right hip, baring his left side to give the doctor access. This would demand the forbearance of a lifetime, as everything inside him wanted to duke it out with this pompous charlatan. Two hands contacted the crown of his pelvis as the doctor checked the healing of his sore joint.

"Any additional pain when I do this?" Bo asked. He pulled Holt's left knee up and put the hip joint through a varied range of motion, from slightly bent to acute.

"Ah, right there, when you brought the knee higher." Holt allowed the words to appease the pain buildup, as he didn't want to seem weak at such close inspection.

"Sure, that's to be expected." Bo stood and backed away, his gaze rigid. "Stand up and let me see you walk."

Holt exhaled a sentence prayer as walking had been next to impossible since the collision. Maybe it was high time he tested his physical abilities, which might have been the doctor's forcible tactic. He set his sights on the kitchen counter and took a step toward it with his right foot. His hip reported the weight shift with stabbing alarm, but he gingerly moved his left foot forward and the pain eased.

"Two more steps," Bo insisted. Holt clamped his fists against his thighs and took the requisite paces. His left hip seemed to be paying penance for his bedlam speed down the mountain—or possibly his surrender at the peak. That didn't mean he had to punish his recovering frame for it now. When the counter came within reach, he leaned on it to ease some weight off the injured joint.

"Good. You can walk now, which brings up my next point." Bo stepped closer and all manner of tolerance dropped from his expression. "I'm suggesting you vacate the premises. Since all strays like to wander, that shouldn't be a problem for you. The truth is—Cami doesn't need you hanging around."

It registered that they had stepped into a more personal arena, one Holt could hold his own in. "Oh? That sounds like an outsider's opinion to me."

"She has friends—long-time friends—that care about her welfare. And that doesn't include the likes of you." Bo bent over him, having a considerable height advantage.

Holt eased out of his proximity and used the sliding glass door handle for a brace. Heat needled up his neck. Discretion had always served him well, but an allusion to Bo's forfeiture of responsibility for Cami's family might be in order here, man to man. He took another step away from the doctor. A flash of pain came and went as he shifted off his left foot. "Here's the thing about staking a claim with an opinion, Doctor Ballard. Since everyone has an opinion, there's little validity in the claim they pose."

Bo straightened as though provoked. His fingers

coiled into a fist. "Since I'm an established doctor in the community and you're something between a failure and riff-raff, I'd say my opinion counts in this regard." A vein bulged on his temple.

It rubbed Holt across the grain that Bo would use his occupation as a trump card. He knew he currently lacked a counter claim, but something came to mind that bore higher relevance—dereliction of duty over time. "Let me see if I can get this math straight, since a doctor can certainly trust numbers. That's eight years of paternal denial times twelve months per year of non-payment of child support. You're approaching one hundred opportunities to make your opinion about Cami's welfare matter, which leaves you the deadbeat dad. In any court of law, that invalidates your claim."

His face reddening as the allegation struck home, Bo came at him fist first with a growl.

Out of nowhere, someone pounded on the sliding glass door demanding his attention. One sideways glance became his mistake as the door slid open and he absorbed a sucker punch right in the mouth. Joyce entered in a fury, shoving her shoe heel into Bo's thigh. A salty flow of blood trickled from Holt's cut lip and he wiped it with the back of his hand, eyes now glued on his opponent.

Bo didn't flinch until Joyce wedged between the two of them, facing him down. "I believe you were just leaving, Bo." Her words dropped like bricks, level and determined.

A tense moment passed before the doctor took a step across the mattress and attempted to regain his false swagger. "Tell Cami no more favors." Bo stormed out of the dining area and grabbed the bag of candy as he left. The front door slammed, cutting the tension in the room.

The cat came in and swirled around Holt's ankle, somehow wicking away his anger and helping him find his composure. His half-victory had a salty taste.

Joyce turned to him and her bluster changed to genuine concern. "Can you get to the bathroom sink?" She placed a caring hand on his elbow. "I'll fix an ice pack while you clean up. I should have known not to trust the two of you in a room alone. Guess my discernment is slipping in my old age."

He nodded and turned toward the laundry room, his hand cupped to catch the blood drips. "At least I can walk now." He lengthened his wincing stride to find the sink and assess the new damage. Cami flashed into his thoughts, but he couldn't let that worry him right now, as she was keeping company with much nicer folks than he'd just encountered.

~

The flat rock under the bridge had been easy to find, and Cami could watch Mitch from the roadside without a commitment to cross the bridge. He had been there a minute or two and no one had come forward. She watched for movement up and down the river, but everyone seemed engaged in recreational activities, fully ignoring her little charity worker. A lump built in her throat and she began to chide herself for being unrealistic in her expectations.

"Lord, there he is—just like you called him—to distribute food to the needy," she prayed across the steering wheel. "Please don't let this be in vain." Tears welled up and she missed the man stepping up to her window until his badge glinted in the sun.

"Is there trouble here, Miss?" He bent to take a look inside as if to find his own answer.

"Just watching my son, officer." She nodded toward the river. "He's trying to cover for Bicycle Man until he comes back, only we didn't know substituting would be this hard. No one's paying any attention to him out there." She tried to filter the disappointment out of her voice, but failed.

He looked over the roof of her car and clicked his tongue. "Oh, I wouldn't say no one."

From under the bridge, a bearded man in a tattered Hawaiian shirt stepped toward the boy. Mitch stiffened. She held her hands over her mouth as the boy smiled and took some of the food out for him. The man held the treasure in his big hands, nodded his thanks, and then returned to the shade of the bridge. Mitch broke into his little victory dance right there on the spot until a bent-backed lady came towards him. The officer chuckled again and patted her shoulder. A tear slid down her cheek as she looked up.

"He'll be fine, just fine," the policeman said. "We all miss Bicycle Man, but maybe this is God's way of having more of us step up. I'll tell the others to watch out for your boy as he makes his rounds. Ask for me, Officer Gaines, if he ever has a moment's trouble."

"I so appreciate that. I had to hover today since it's his first day out but he's on his own after this. His loop includes the trailer park up on the river, and then three loading docks on Industry Road. He's fine with it all. I'm the one having to grow up a little."

"Your half-pint's giving you permission to go have a life, so make the most of it," he replied. With a tip of his hat he departed, leaving her to think about her time commitments and how she could fashion more of a life out of them. Holt seeped into the progression of her thoughts and wouldn't disappear, no matter how much she tried to think of something else.

~

Joyce exchanged Holt's original ice pack with a replacement. "Cami will be more than a little surprised when she sees your lip."

He surrendered the melted one and pressed the fresh one against his new tender spot, swollen in protest. "Yeah, I don't know why I tripped over Scrubs like that." He rolled his eyes in an attempt to sell the fib. "Maybe I'm a klutz and never knew it."

She wagged a finger at him. "Honesty is always the best policy."

He leaned away from the bar in the office chair. Of course he would have to admit the foul blow that led to the brawl. Man enough to take that blame, the paternity revelation had him more concerned.

"I figured something out, Joyce. Bo is Mitch's father. The resemblance is unmistakable—the earlobes, the hairline. Does Bo go as far back as Cami's nursing school days?"

She turned fully toward him so that her shoulders formed a protective blockade. Still awash in disbelief, her nod came very slowly. "You're treading on broken glass here, my friend. If Cami wants us to know who Mitch's father is, she'll tell us herself. Accusations would be both speculative and unwise."

"Not to mention judgmental, which I am not." Holt leaned forward and rested the ice pack on the counter, then lowered his cheek so it made weightless contact with his busted lip. "Bo caused some trouble at the clinic earlier this week. Cami had a patient run out in tears from under his care. There might be a patterned behavior surfacing here that wrenches my gut every time I think about it. She's very uneasy about what happened and I have a feeling she's not going to cover up for him anymore."

Joyce shifted, as though her shoes were tight. "Well, that certainly puts things in a different light. Maybe there's a way to formalize an investigation to collect similar allegations, you know, through the clinic's non-profit board or something."

When her fingertips alighted on his shoulder, Holt realized Joyce would be a strong ally if he wanted to move forward. "It all comes down to Cami." He lifted his head off the ice pack to look at her. "She has to step toward the truth if we're going to help her. Exposing Bo is one thing, but bringing their history back into the spotlight won't make the decision easy for her."

"Maybe if she has the support she needs, she could be brave. Never underestimate what a woman will do for those she loves."

"Joyce, you make a great sounding board, you know that? Are you sure you want to go to Maine and leave us here to figure this out for ourselves?"

"Most definitely." Her lips pulled into a thin smile as if the shore drew her away.

~

The trailer park had been an immediate success, and Mitch became more generous, in her opinion. Cami watched as he placed what was left of the donations on the third loading dock. He had completed the full loop. She exited the car and released the latch on the hatchback.

Mitch rode over with stars in his eyes. "That was awesome." He dismounted and transferred the bike to her hands. "I can hardly wait for next week."

"Let's see what Holt thinks about a schedule." She wrestled the handlebars closer to the hatch. "Bicycle Man probably tried to keep it regular so folks knew when to expect him."

"Will I be on my own next week, Mom?"

"More than likely, Mitch. I trust you and know you'll do the best job possible. Now let's get back home and tackle those homework assignments. I bet Holt will be starving by the time I get dinner made."

"You know what, Mom?" The boy plopped down in the passenger's seat while she hoisted the bike into the back. "I think you like taking care of Holt. I like him, too. He's nice."

"Well, I hope you won't mind him for a next-door neighbor, because Aunt Joyce has offered to let him stay at her place this summer while she's gone."

"Way cool. Hey, maybe we could fix up his bicycle over the summer—when I'm not at the pool, that is."

She got in and couldn't hide her smile that he was already making plans with Holt in the center, because she had caught herself doing the same thing.

"Sounds like a guy project," she replied. "Now buckle up and let's head back to find out how he's doing. Bo was supposed to check his hip while we've been gone, so he might be good as new." A lighthearted feeling overwhelmed her as the car looped around and headed for home.

~

Holt pulled a length of garden hose, borrowing from Joyce's side of the duplex, and watered Cami's foundation plantings. He drenched some much-neglected plants with their first drink of water in a long while. Being outside equaled good medicine, though he still walked with a slight limp. Recovery had a wholesome quality to it—not a rush of overactive hyperbole, but a steady step-by-step comeback. Surrounded by good people, he was getting the help he needed, so it only seemed natural to help in return.

He caught the calico cat peering out the picture window and couldn't resist the boyish impulse to spray at it with the hose. He gave the spot a spritz and the cat reared on its hind legs, patting at the water as it spattered on the windowpane. Laughing out loud, he almost missed the glint of olive green reflected in the glass. He turned and caught sight of Cami's car on the driveway with her at the wheel, jaw dropping at the sight of him out in her front yard.

"Hey Holt." Mitch waved across his mother.

The car stopped and he waved back as he pulled the hose to its full extension to water the last bush. The boy arrived in a wink of the eye and drank from the spout. Cami rushed up to him and when he turned toward her, the shock of his new injury ricocheted across her face. He relinquished the hose to the boy. Her fingers seemed eager to trace the new line of demarcation requiring her nursing skills. He intended to stop at nibbling her fingertips, but before he could help it, playful affection skyrocketed. He soon had her in a full hug right there in the front yard. Pain that pulsated from the new wound came like a secondary nuisance. With Cami applied like a healing compress, he let the sensation wash over him as a resurrected man, alive and standing solidly on his own two feet.

Chapter 7

Her heart light with companionship, Cami made quick work of the dinner dishes. She washed the spaghetti smears down the disposal and slid the sponge over the counter. When she invaded his territory, Holt pulled back the notebook paper and let her clean. She flashed him a slight smile but refused to look at him. Having him across the bar served as distraction enough.

"We've got to crack down on this ad campaign." Mitch cleared his throat like a chairman of the board. He slid off his bar stool and stepped over to the refrigerator, where he paused to read the flyer again.

Cami glanced over and assessed his level of contemplation as she scrubbed the range top clean. "Read it again out loud, honey. Let's give Holt all the information he needs to help you come up with the best slogan ever." This time she allowed her gaze to glide over to him and their eyes met in mutual admiration. She hadn't planned for the blush, so she tried to hide it back at the sink while Mitch read the challenge. She found a spoon in the suds and rescued it from oblivion as the disposal garbled down the remnants of their Italian feast.

Holt folded his hands together like a sage advisor. "I'm thinking that today's food run may give you a different angle on Save Always grocery store than most people have."

Mitch approached his seat and stopped, deep in contemplation.

Cami slid the tea towel across the oven door handle and leaned against the counter's rim. "You could say that they feed everyone, since we learned today that it doesn't matter if you paid or not."

Mitch tapped the pencil eraser against the countertop, his mind busy working over the delivery experience.

Holt turned toward her and moved his index finger over his lip in a secret signal.

She replied with a wink. That warm feeling came back again, the one that started in her chest and radiated out every time he looked at her. This time she didn't try to squelch it. She enjoyed the tingling sensation.

"True, they are feeding everybody. But there's more to it than that," Mitch said, steeped in thought. "They've been doing this for years, but what really sticks out to me is that they feed us every day. Does that make any sense?"

Holt busied himself writing headings on a blank sheet of paper.

"I think you're onto something key there, Mitchell-the-marketing-pro," she replied. "You've had a close-up look at people who only get to eat what's provided each day, so maybe that will lend you a unique perspective."

Holt held up the paper to challenge the boy. "Here's what I want you to do, Mitch. I've made two columns for you to brainstorm under. One says 'Feeding' and the other says 'Frequency.' Marketing is all about the words you pitch. They have to flow together like a river of expression. I want you to come up with at least six ways to say both aspects—first, that everybody gets fed, and second, the significance of how frequently that has to happen. Then we can cross-match the phrases and come up with the absolute best combination for your entry."

Mitch's face brightened. "Awesome, Holt!" He took the paper in his chubby hand and regarded the challenge set before him. "Must find a quieter place to think." He slipped out of the room.

Cami looked at Holt, her brow arched in wonder. She slid her hand across the bar and laid it on top of Holt's, as a silent thanks for his inspiration. "You want to tell me how you got your split lip, now that we're alone?" She lowered her face to close the distance between them.

He touched the swollen epicenter of her inquiry with his free hand.

She traced the movement with her gaze. "Are you accident-prone? Maybe I should know that about you." Her tone carried a tease as the cat swirled around the bottom of his bar stool and distracted him.

When he looked back, a devilish glint twinkled in his eyes. "Maybe I'm more confrontational than klutzy." His smile pulled against the lip tear. "The doctor and I had a go-around, which sparked like a powder-keg into an explosive blow."

Astonishment swept through her as she processed his confession. Cami braced forward on her elbows. "More details, please."

"He asked me to drop down on the mattress for the hip check, which I did. And afterward, I took several pain-filled steps at his request to prove my gait. Guess the doctor didn't like the way I walk." Holt smirked.

Something seemed missing in his brief explanation. "Okay, what else are you leaving out? That gleam in your eyes gives you away."

"I had to fend off his personal suggestion that I scram and leave your family alone," he replied. "It didn't strike me as medical advice, so I found a way to question the validity of his opinion."

She squinted her eyes, expecting more information.

He diverted his gaze for several moments and then locked onto her stare again. "I took a couple of steps back when Bo turned ballistic. The next thing I knew, Joyce banged on the back door trying to break it up. When I glanced over at her, he leveled me with a punch right in the mouth. Hence the split lip following the doctor-approved hip, which might be considered one step forward and a tiny slip back."

She pulled erect on her side of the counter. "What did Aunt Joyce do?"

"She wedged her wafer-thin self between us like a UN ambassador. She strongly suggested to Bo that he should leave, and after a few tense moments, he took the hint, grabbed the gummy candy he had brought for Mitch, and stormed out with a threat on his lips."

"What'd he say?" She crossed her arms on her chest to keep from quivering.

"Tell Cami no more favors." He held his palms up to accentuate the delivery. "The next thing I know, I'm headed to the bathroom dripping blood while Joyce fixes the ice pack."

"You can walk again. Tell me how that feels…"

"Like getting permission to live again," he replied. "Well, that and some other things added to it." He rose from the barstool.

Cami experienced an off-balance sensation as though she was toeing a cliffhanger. She moved around the bar to follow him and they met alongside the dinette table.

"Other things like what?" Her hands found the crown of her hips and they stood like that for half a minute in some kind of emotional standoff.

"I only make confessions like that under the soft duress of candlelight," he replied, but the look in his eyes gave him away.

For the first time in her life, Cami wished that time would move forward just a little, as the day had plenty of natural light remaining.

"Holt, can you come help me?" Mitch called from a distant location.

Holt's face brightened and he made a dismissive bow. "Duty calls, but I shall return." His gaze lingered on her face.

"Great, so maybe I can get some housework done around here and not have to spend my day off tomorrow scrubbing boy-dirt from the premises."

"Count your blessings. Where are you, Mitch?" He headed for the hall.

"In my room, the door on the right."

Cami shook her head at the reminder for gratitude, and now she felt doubly blessed having two mess-makers to clean up after. Grabbing the wet tea towel, she stepped into the laundry room and spent the next half hour becoming reacquainted with their dirty laundry.

With one load now in the dryer, she walked out to presoak a bloody hand towel in the sink and caught movement in the hallway. Holt and Mitch had hauled his sickbed mattress back to its original location without so much as consulting her.

She ran the faucet to fill the sink. "What's going on in there?"

"I'm moving into Mitch's room for these last few days," Holt replied. "So we can get your household back to normal."

She appreciated the gesture, though she would miss their routine of saying goodnight. She stepped into the vacated dining area and pulled a couple of large houseplants back into place in front of the patio door. The candle sat on the edge of the counter, as though to mock her. She grabbed it in retaliation, moved it into the living room, and centered it on the old trunk she had repurposed for a coffee table.

Holt dusted his hands off as if signaling his readiness for the next task. "I'll mop the floor before we move the table back under the chandelier."

She glanced up at him, her mouth gaping open at his offer to assist with domestic work.

He blew a breath to play her as a feather knocked over. "Let me check the laundry room for the aforementioned mop." He disappeared into the kitchen.

Mitch appeared, waggling the paper in his hand. "Mom, I have my final slogan entry."

"Let's hear it, buddy." She braced her leg against the trunk to steady herself.

"Save Always Grocery—feeding the Golden community one day at a time." He beamed with pride at the end result.

In two steps she had him smothered in a hug. A faint whistle rose from the dining area, echoed by the swish of a mop as she kissed the boy's hair in an overflow of pure gratitude.

~

Holt enjoyed the play of candlelight off the picture window while Cami put Mitch to bed. Worried he hadn't left her enough room to sit, he slid down on the overstuffed sofa and patted the cushion upon her arrival.

She smiled and came toward him. "Hope we haven't lost the ambiance we enjoyed in the other room." She sat down a comfortable distance from him. Murmur from the TV filled the background.

He gestured toward the flickering candle. "Oh, I don't know how we could. I still need my nurse, even if I'm graduating out of my sick bed."

She fixed her hair in what looked like nervous response. "*Your* nurse?" A glint of mischief flickered in her eyes.

He shifted toward her, feigning deeper thought by creasing his brow. "Let me recall how it went. Oh, yes. Blur of mountainside, crash of olive green, angel bent over me and hatchback rescue. Soft mattress, scratched hide, angry hip, and busted lip." He inched over toward her again, unable to blink. "Nights of scripture wisdom, flicker of candlelight, sweet powder scent, and the same heavenly angel bent over me." The cadence of his words extended the moment, as his lips grew mutinous in their quest to forego language for something higher, but he controlled his physical impulse to make sure she had made the transition with him.

"Your explanation sounds a little like poetry." She tilted her head as if a changed perspective would provide further insight.

He caught her hand and pressed it against his chest so she could feel the sincerity. "Words spoken from the heart tend to take on their own rhythm. Tonight, our friendship moves to a more mutual place, where I don't have to be bleeding and you don't have to touch me, unless you want to." At that, he released his hand from hers and waited to see if it would stay on his chest or retreat.

Her warm touch lingered and then inched across his collarbone to the back of his neck. "*Your* nurse," she repeated, only sweeter this time, as though she finally liked the sound of it. She pulled him closer.

He relented to the good work his lips had hungered for and delivered the kiss at her invitation. Time went liquid within that place of mutual tenderness as he lost himself in the sensation.

She finally pulled back for a breath "Well then, Holt Ellis. I've been wondering if you could tell me about Bicycle Man and how it came about that he went missing?"

Pierced in a moment of complete vulnerability, he took her arrow of inquiry right in the bull's-eye of his heart. Now where could he hide?

~

Cami knew she had led him into a sensitive disclosure and wanted to encourage him. "Would you say he didn't go away all at once?" She turned her shoulder and nestled back against him, allowing his arm to cradle her there. She laid her head back and gave him time to collect his story.

"Yes, you could say that. It started with his layoff from full-time employment almost fifteen months ago. That trickled into part-time work both here and in Denver. He took the light rail into LoDo for six months, and then that ad agency went belly up in the recession, so it was off to more part time, less creative whatever."

"Does Bicycle Man have a degree in marketing?" She wondered where Holt got his knowledge base since he seemed to be exceptional at it.

"Stamped with the University of Colorado's gold seal of approval. Which only goes to show that a diploma doesn't guarantee anything when the economy tanks."

She wanted to hear more. "So Bicycle Man's been struggling for awhile, has he?"

Holt rested his cheek against her hair as the rest of the story floated toward the surface. "He lightened up his possessions, cut his expenses, and kept working for next to nothing just to eat and weather the storm. That's when the homeless circuit started in earnest."

"Bet he had real empathy for the down-and-outers from that vantage point."

"Yes, he most certainly did. But the payback was phenomenal, being the go-between man. The store donated everything and all Bicycle Man had to do was deliver it."

"And let me guess. The people somehow got under

his thinning hide and made life worthwhile."

"That halted the downward spiral for a long time, but winter comes as a merciless haunt when you don't have enough to eat. Depression probably contributed to the abysmal situation and by the time spring came, he just couldn't pull out of it."

She placed a hand on his arm and the unpadded surface it landed on testified to the authenticity of the story. When he fell quiet, she began to recognize what a miracle this moment represented.

"I honestly don't know what would have happened to me if you had bypassed me that day on the mountain."

Cami tried to grow comfortable with all the sharp-edged disclosure the night had brought. "My story seems to reflect more of a dormancy than a slow fade, but the effect is the same, life sucking and heart numbing every step you take."

"I put my life under God's will at the top of the mountain that day," Holt whispered through her hair. "God causes everything to change. Only he can transform someone from the heart outward. Of course, you have to be willing to let him."

The TV shifted from programming into commercial, causing the volume to jump. Cami sat up in rigid recognition at the picture that unfolded on the screen in front of her. The happy hostess of the only Mexican restaurant in town happened to be her mountain-climbing friend with the broken ankle. She blinked as a stab of conviction pierced her deep inside. "I'm having another God-led moment as he's allowed me to spy the victimized girl from the clinic. By any chance, do you like chimichangas?"

Chapter 8

olt sat at Cami's computer trying to adjust to her ergonomic mouse. True to his word, he endeavored to recreate his resume to highlight his former accomplishments and attempt to connect the employment stints so that no major lapses were evident. Above all else, he would keep it truthful, as this was his life in condensed form and he had a backbone of integrity, though it didn't have much else hanging on it right now.

Being honest with himself, he enjoyed the marketing homework assignments Mitch had brought him. That type of representation remained his passion and he liked to think he was somewhat good at it. The boy seemed to pick up on the spirit of pitching an ad, which made him smile. Cami's focused attention seemed to benefit her son, leaving him inspired to contribute what he could. Funny, he'd never thought much about parenting, yet here he could chip in without so much as a hesitation. Talk about a crazy turn of events.

The sliding door opened and Cami stepped in from the patio, shared by both halves of the duplex. He typed in the last part time job he'd held and clicked on the "save" button before she could distract him.

"How's the packing going at Joyce's?" He moved the file onto the desktop. When no reply came, he looked up and realized that something had shattered the young woman who had gone next door less than an hour ago. Her eyes were rimmed with red.

Restless, she pulled out a chair and joined him at the patio table. "I…want to take you out to lunch today," she began, her words shaky.

"You don't need to do that." The extra expense seemed over the top.

"Please, there's a reason I have to go. Remember last night I saw the girl who ran from the clinic? She serves as the hostess for that Mexican restaurant near Main Street."

"Well, what if she isn't there today?"

"I can check again tonight or maybe tomorrow. I really have to talk to her."

"You mean to find out what happened inside of that exam room?" He watched her squirm a bit before she regained her composure to answer.

"Yes, I have to know because there's something that feels wrong and I have to search it out. This is something…deeply personal for me. I have to ask you to trust me and be willing to go with me."

"I'm more than willing." He closed the laptop to accent his decision. "And I have a cheap fondness for a chimichanga with good guacamole by its side." When she snickered at his culinary confession, he slid his hand across the table. "Don't be afraid of going down that mountain, Cami."

"God will have to help me, because this is hard." She laid her head on the tabletop.

"Father, help Cami step toward righteousness as she tries to right a wrong." He rose to his feet and closed the distance between them. When he laid his hand on her shoulder, a sob shook her body and the crying resumed. "Help heal our hearts as only you can do, Lord. Fix us with your tender mercy. In the holy name of Jesus, we pray. Amen." He gripped her shoulder in solidarity. Holt knew how deep hurt could run. Backbone deep.

~

A well-patched stucco façade greeted them as the name "El Cantina" glared in red lettering over a low-hanging arch. Cami nodded as Holt held the door for her and stepped inside, allowing a second to let her eyes adjust to the dark interior. Leafy plants spilled out of terra cotta pots and found enjoyment across trellises shaped like fans. A peace settled over her as she looked expectantly for the wait staff to greet them. Holt stepped into view and gave her a little wink of assurance as delightful aromas emerged from the bustling kitchen. Someone in uniform backed out of the saloon-style door with an oversized tub in her hands. Barely clear of the swinging door, the tub slipped and headed toward the floor, causing the employee to gasp. Holt managed a saving grab along the tub's rim and the load of napkin-rolled flatware was spared a close encounter with the not-so-sanitary-looking floor.

"Thank you so much," the hostess gushed. "That would have been an extra hour's work for me." She hauled the tub around to the hostess station and Cami glimpsed her familiar face. She mentally rehearsed the plan she and Holt had discussed, allowing herself only a brief mention of their earlier encounter.

"Hey, glad to see you're wearing a bootie on that ankle. That should keep you from running down another mountain anytime soon."

"Oh my goodness, it's you, the nurse from the clinic." She brushed her hair behind her ear. A stocky Hispanic man walked by slowly, casting an eye at their exchange.

Holt wrapped Cami's shoulder in a slight hug. "A table for two, please."

"Of course, sir. Right this way." She grabbed two folded menus from a rack and led them back toward a private little corner past a dormant fireplace. Bright Mexican scenery scrolled across the painted walls. "Your server should be right with you." She placed the menus on the table. "It really is great to see you again. I'll try to be the kind of patient you'd be proud of."

"You already are, sweetie." Cami slid onto the left bench as Holt sat across from her. "Hey, why don't you stop by and see us a little later if you're not too busy."

A cloud passed over the woman's face as she turned and retreated to the front.

"Did you see that last look?" Cami's voice held a quiver.

"Hard to miss it," he replied, unfolding the menu. "Ah, there it is. Number sixteen, the killer chimichanga. How about you, Cami? What would you like today?"

"For starters, I'd like my stomach to stop knotting

up."

"Look, if we don't appear to be enjoying ourselves, she might not come back."

"Good point. I'm out at a restaurant not having to eat my own cooking on a rare day off. That should be reason enough to celebrate right there."

"You're a pretty good cook, if I do say so myself." He lowered the menu. "My ribs don't seem to be poking out any more." His eyes smiled as he returned his attention to the menu. "What about the burrito combo? It seems most reasonably priced, and if it's too much food, you can take some back home to Mitch."

"Now you're helping me avoid the next wave of guilt for going out to eat without him."

"Something tells me you're doing this for his sake too, not to splurge and be self-indulgent." Holt closed the menu.

She straightened in her seat and an ounce of relief crept in that broke the tension she'd been carrying around since last night. A shorthaired waitress approached and whipped out her order pad. Before she could open her mouth, Holt took charge.

"She'd like the beef burrito combo and I'll have a number sixteen. Can you bring some chips and salsa while we wait?"

"Yes, sir. Coming right up." The waitress jotted down the order and disappeared around the corner.

"No one ever cared enough to order for me before," Cami admitted, her face softening.

"Hope I did the right thing." Holt released the seal on his napkin and unrolled his flatware, laying it on the placemat.

"If not, I'm switching plates with you." She

chuckled under her breath and touched her foot to his calf under the table.

"My chimi!" His hands crossed his chest. "So close and yet so far away."

The server arrived with the chips and salsa so Cami waited until they were alone again. She pursed her lips and gave him a protracted look.   "You know, this is starting to feel like a real date." She connected with his calf again.

Holt ran his hand over his cleanly shaven face where a fingertip paused on the split lip. "I thought it was a real date." His brow arched for emphasis. "After all, aren't you the one saving Bicycle Man?" He dipped a tortilla chip, crunched it in his mouth, and savored the taste out loud.

A little joy bubbled up inside Cami and expressed itself as a laugh. "Oh yes. I guess I am." Though salvation might have worked the other way around, his unguarded candor put her at ease. When he shoved the salsa bowl toward her, she helped herself to the crispy appetizer with open abandon.

~

A sense of deep satisfaction saturated his pores as Holt studied the remains of his delectable lunch, confined in a cozy booth with such a beautiful woman. "Since this outing could be mistaken for a date, may I tell you how incredible it feels to be here with you today?"

Cami stopped pushing the rice around on her plate, her far-away look dissipating in a faint smile. "You're just flying high off that guacamole." She smothered a grin with her napkin.

Unable to take his gaze from hers, interest flared to

heat when her foot stroked against his calf again. Smolder from the contact crept upwards.

"Maybe—and maybe not." He reached for her hand across the table just as their hobbling hostess returned.

"I'm officially on break for the next fifteen minutes, so I thought I'd come back and see how my favorite nurse was doing," the hostess said. "I'm Lyric Baldwin, by the way."

"Cami Walsh," she replied. "And this is another friend I met the same day I met you, Lyric. This is Holt Ellis." He nodded and offered his hand as the hostess scanned his scratched exterior. "Yeah, the mountain tried to shred him up too, but I had to intervene."

"You ladies will have to excuse me as I limp my way to recovery by way of the men's room." Holt slid out of the booth, agreeable to implement the plan they had devised earlier but ruing the disruptive timing of it. Things had just started getting cozy. He followed the signage and found the restrooms beyond the beverage service area while he examined the feeling that lingered in his gut. He knew better than to think it was a guacamole high. No, not at all.

~

Cami motioned to the now-empty bench. "Can we have a little girl-to-girl talk?"

The girl glanced down the aisle and then buckled herself into the tight space, dragging her bootie underneath the table's protection. Her face blanched white but her eyes held a trace of conviction.

"Let me be truthful about the problem that's emerging at the medical clinic." She leaned forward, having directed the conversation toward the trouble spot they both shared. "We suspect a staff member might be behaving unprofessionally, so we need to have the problem examined and addressed by our board of directors. In order to do that, I need to document these unfortunate encounters and provide the board with the evidence they need to rectify the situation." When Lyric tightened her lips, the booth turned into a sauna.

"First, I should admit to you that I am also a victim, but have delayed reporting it, and I let the despicable deed eat me alive for eight years."

A look of shock flitted across the young woman's face.

"This person is choosing to usurp his authority and violate patient's rights at the same time, which equates to a gross miscarriage of justice, one that we can no longer stand for."

The hostess shifted uncomfortably on the bench, like she might bolt from the premises.

"Listen, when I saw your face with all the tears that day in the clinic, my own dreadful experience resurfaced, and it reopened in a fresh new way." Cami nodded and held her gaze. "I wondered how many times this has to happen before someone finally puts a stop to it. I cried and I prayed. That's when I knew I had to do something about it myself. When I saw your picture on the TV commercial last night, I knew that this was my chance. So I'm here to ask you, won't you please help me get this ugliness out into the light?"

The woman sat motionless, betrayed only by the tear that declared mutiny down her cheek. "I'll help you if it means no one else has to suffer his advances like we did." Lyric looked away, unable to meet her gaze.

Cami found her courage mounting with their

combined strength and withdrew an envelope from her purse. "Take this form and write out what happened, describing his actions and your reaction as it transpired." She slid the folded sheet across the table. It wedged against the doggie bag like some leftover thought until the hostess pulled it into her apron pocket. "It's addressed to me, and I've also put a slip of paper inside with my phone number on it, if you ever want to talk."

She looked around as though trouble lurked nearby. "What happens next?"

Moved by the young woman's wounded innocence, Cami knew she was on the right trail at last. "Justice happens." She caught sight of Holt returning up the aisle.

"I'm sure you'll be filling out one of these, too." Lyric slipped from the seat to return to her shift.

Cami hesitated a moment but knew she could not disappoint her new sister-in-suffering. "You can count on it." Her voice rose to make certain of the delivery.

Holt nodded as the hostess passed him and he stood by the table with a questioning expression on his face.

"She'll do it. I mean, we'll do it." She slid out as he dropped a tip for the waitress and handed the rest of the cash back to her.

The manager appeared down the aisle. "I hope you've enjoyed your dining experience today."

Holt turned to retrieve the doggie bag and Cami flashed a genuine smile, stuffing the bills into her purse. "Totally enjoyable, both the food and your staff." She gestured to the front of the restaurant. "We hope to come again soon."

Holt hoisted the leftovers and added his two cents.

"And please give our regards to the wonderful cooks in the kitchen that created this magnificent chimichanga." The stuffy manager broke into a chuckle and tossed a slight wave in response to the compliment.

Cami started to wing Holt with her elbow but realized he was too scratched up to pick on. She, however, felt more whole with every step toward justice.

On the trip out to her car, Holt seemed distracted by the urban vista of downtown Golden. "Hey, do you think you could loan me an hour of your time?" His question floated over the roof of her car. "I have some friends I'd like you to meet." He opened the passenger door and pitched the doggie bag inside for safekeeping.

"We have until three-thirty when the school bus pulls into Valley Vista. I'm all yours until then." Though it sounded like a tease, Cami meant every word.

Chapter 9

Holt stood on the Main Street Bridge looking out over the silver-rushing waters of Clear Creek. With Cami nestled beside him against the rail, he let the sun fill him with redemptive purpose. "I've come to love this place. Thanks for encouraging me to compile my resume again. Funny how you can look back and see how everything has led up to this point, isn't it?"

"A perfect plan set in place by the hand of God." She tightened her grip on his elbow, the mountains vaulting up from the edge of town. "Why do you suppose we never met before? I've been here for almost ten years and our paths didn't cross."

He watched as several sparrows flew onto the flat rock below, searching for food. "No, not until I really needed you out of my desperation. Or maybe because I finally relinquished myself fully to God."

"Or because it was high time that I fixed my plight and God sent you to give me the right motivation." She pulled closer, the sunlight playing off her features.

Leaning in, he rubbed noses with her, resisting the magnetic urge to kiss her right there.

"Hey, break it up." A figure stepped up behind them on the bridge. "No public display of affection on my shift."

Holt detected a trace of tease in the reprimand as he turned around to find an officer of the law staring them down. The man studied them both and then the light of recognition flashed across his face.

"Why, you're the mother of our Junior Bicycle Man." He offered his hand to Cami. "Looks like you've taken my advice to find a life."

"Yes sir, Officer Gaines," she replied. "This is my friend, Holt Ellis."

The officer examined Holt's scraped exterior and tilted his head in scrutiny. "What happened to you?"

"I had a mountain chew me up and spit me out," Holt replied, determined to keep his story short and sweet. As an afterthought, he allowed a smile to chase the explanation.

The man chuckled and tipped his hat, his eyes twinkling. "We look forward to having our Bicycle Man back, of course, but until then, I've got my boys watching out for your pint-sized version. You two have a splendid weekend."

"Thank you, sir." Holt pulled Cami back to his side as if to recreate the previous intimacy. He waited until the officer had strolled off the bridge before he turned to her with a little ribbing.

"So Junior Bicycle Man is only on the job for a day

and already has his support system in place?" He touched his forehead to hers.

"Well, we were a bit pathetic in our debut, which garnered us some added attention."

"It feels good to have the community take notice, I have to admit. Now, how about you follow me down the path under the bridge to meet some of my old friends?"

"Lead on, as any friends of yours need to become friends of mine."

Where the sidewalk hooked up at the end of the bridge's arching span, he tugged her onto a well-worn path that led under the first set of support pillars. Their approach seemed to startle the residents below. He slowed as his eyes adjusted to the dimness of the nether-realm. "Lucy?" He searched for his favorite homeless lady. Instead, a massive Hawaiian print shirt appeared in formidable fashion.

"Who's that askin'?" a woman replied.

"It's Bicycle Man." He squeezed Cami's hand. The tropical blockade gave way to reveal a bent-backed woman, made haggard by the hardships of life. "How've you been?"

"Hungry when you didn't show up. That's how." She stepped closer to him with an uneven gait. "But things are better now. A boy came and brought the food." She hobbled up in front of him and took in his scarred face and arm, clucking as she made her assessment.

"That's my little boy." Cami tapped her chest with the admission. "His name is Mitchell and he's pretty excited to take on the job while Bicycle Man is recovering."

"Lucy, this is my friend—and my nurse—Cami Walsh. I wanted you to meet her."

"I see." The woman shifted to size up a new target of scrutiny. "Fell for your nurse, did you?"

"I was in a right pathetic way."

Cami shifted closer so their shoulders touched and the sensation set off a buzz in Holt's head. "No, I fell for him, Miss Lucy, if you want to know the whole truth."

The old woman leaned on her walking stick and moved back toward her guardian. "We all fell for him, Sugar. We all did, once upon awhile ago."

Holt let her confession wash over his heart as he nodded to the tall man by the pillar. "Leroy, spread the word that the boy will be back on his rounds on Tuesday." Holt pulled Cami back out into the light of an increasingly beautiful day as the man wagged his fingers in silent compliance. "Walk up the creek to the trailer park with me."

She leaned on his good side. "That would be delightful."

"So you fell in love with me first? Well, that was remarkable news to yours truly." He shielded his eyes as they walked onto the bridge's pedestrian path to better see her reaction. Cami feigned distraction by water play down below as a raft floated by without its owner. "Hey, maybe while we're walking out here in the pure sunlight we could be honest about what's happening between us." He slowed his pace to regain her attention.

"Suppose you start with yourself."

"That's fair enough. I'm filling up on the inside, ever since I regained consciousness in your home under your care. That voice, that touch, that powdery smell at night…they all linger on my mind until I can hardly think of anything else."

"From a nurse's perspective, your reaction sounds viral." She teased with her tone. "You might have to get treated for that type of outbreak."

He tugged her hand to cross the street on the far side of the bridge where shade greeted them along the creek's west bank. A strolling path followed the bank and meandered behind civic buildings—the library, the police station, and the town's pioneer museum. Statuary caught his eye and he decided to pause a minute under the shade at one of the public accesses. When Cami wandered down the slate steps to stand on natural river rock, his mind's eye took a picture.

The combination of the creek's constant sweep and her lithe beauty overcame his hesitation and the right words came bubbling up. "Cami Walsh, listen to me." He stood on the top step looking down at her. The aqueous gurgle of the creek gave him permission to speak as she gazed up at him, her skirt flouncing in the breeze. "I'm falling in love with you. I want you to hear it first and then I want the entire world to know. You make me want to live again. I want to fill my days with you."

A light round of applause emanated from the museum's back patio where several couples were enjoying a late lunch together. Though a blush raced up her neck, his gaze locked on the promise of love he saw in her eyes. He met her halfway to the creek and wrapped her in a hug that filled his arms with the object of his growing desire.

"Holt, I have a major gap I need to close up before

I can speak to you regarding matters of the heart," she whispered into his ear.

"And I fully respect that." He stroked her cheeks with his thumbs and soaked in her porcelain features, which set off a tremor inside. "Now you know how I feel, so there's no question of my intent."

"No, there's no question," she repeated. "Why don't we stay on safer ground and find these upstream friends of yours?"

"And Cami hatches yet another great idea." He pulled her back up to the trail. After a relatively straight run, the creek took a sharp bend westward and looped around a rocky outcrop, opening out where rows of mobile homes hugged the bank. A small, modest community thrived here, independent and cooperatively sharing the confined waterfront space. A couple of familiar figures resting at a sheltered picnic table with a game of checkers sprawled between them.

Holt stepped up to the pavilion at the trailer park entrance. "How's it going, fellas?"

"Well, well, well. Look at what the chickens scratched up," the broad-shouldered man said with a toothless smile.

"Scratched up are the right words," his skinny opponent replied with a laugh.

"Tom and Donnie, this is my friend Cami. She's been nursing me back to health since I decided to come down the mountain without my bike under me."

"Rough way to make an acquaintance," Donnie added.

"Pleased to meet you, ma'am. I'm Big Tom, at your service." The heavy man swept his baseball cap through the air.

"And I'm Donnie, the winner of this game." The thin man hopped his game piece through a heavy blockade to reach the back line. His moustache twitched with the victory.

"I'm the mother of the young boy who delivered the groceries yesterday." Cami stepped closer with the introduction. "His name is Mitchell, but he goes by Mitch."

"Glad to have him come by," Tom said with a nod. "We didn't know you were laid up, Bicycle Man, but I like your replacement just the same. That boy's got gumption."

"That he does. I'm on the mend now, as Cami is my nurse and she's doing some miracle work on me."

"Well, maybe I should come down the mountain the rough way," Donnie replied.

"Sorry man, but this particular nurse is taken." Holt saluted his farewell and turned Cami toward the creek. They wandered out to the rocky point where bedrock insisted on making the stream turn. The water tore against the rocks and cascaded down several rough drops, giving the local kayakers a risk-filled enhancement through which to maneuver.

Cami sat on the cap of a rock, seemingly mesmerized by the current. "Powerful isn't it?"

Holt examined her feminine profile against the raw force of nature transporting the melt-water, and a sensation washed through his chest. *Carved by the hand of God.* He etched the scene to memory for a remembrance of the day he first confessed his love at the water's edge.

~

Cami stood in the kitchen, her full attention on her

dejected son.

Mitch tossed his backpack into the living room corner. "My teacher hasn't heard anything back from the slogan contest. This weekend might drag on forever until I find out the results."

"Maybe God's trying to teach you patience." She peeled an apple for his afternoon snack.

"Wasn't that my lesson just last week?" the boy complained. "Hey, where's Holt?"

"Guess I wore him out walking along the creek in downtown Golden today." A smile wandered onto her face at the memory of his love declaration. "He's in your room taking a short nap, so try to keep it down. Okay?"

"Sure thing, Mom. I'm glad he's getting better. He was kind of scary at first, coming here so messed up." He stepped into the kitchen to wash his hands at the sink.

"We're supposed to be tenderhearted to all God's children, aren't we?"

"Some are easier than others, like Holt."

"Yes, he makes it easy to care about him. At least I think so."

"Tell me, Mom. How did Holt know how to draw me that map for the food dropoff for the homeless? Do you think he knows Bicycle Man?"

Her thoughts skipped through possibilities on how to bridge the subject while she walked to the refrigerator and pulled down the newspaper clipping. She brought it to the sink where Mitch dried his hands and presented it to him in the plain light of day.

"Does the man in that picture look familiar?" She looked closer and now recognized Big Tom and Donnie in the shot as well. She held her peace, hoping he'd come to the truth himself.

The boy took the article into his hands and studied it, his eyes squinting. "I'm not sure." He shook his head. "It just doesn't make sense that Bicycle Man would give up on the homeless people and leave them like that."

"Honey, look at me." Cami drew her son toward her. "He didn't leave them to starve on purpose. Bicycle Man had an unavoidable accident. I'm sure he's trying very hard to come back."

"What are you trying to tell me, Mom? I don't get it." The boy's eyes grew wide and he glanced back at the photo hoping to see more clearly this time.

"Our new friend, Holt, is Bicycle Man. Trust me, Mitch." She clamped her hands tighter on his shoulders. "It's Holt, honey. And he can't come back yet because Mommy knocked him off the road, crushed his bike, and now is trying the very best she knows how to help him get all better."

From the boy's expression, her revelation translated into something unacceptable in an instant. Mitch shoved the clipping onto the counter and tore out of her grip. He ran through the dining area and out the front door, causing it to bang in objection in his wake.

She followed him as far as the doorway to see what direction he had headed, and managed a sigh of relief that he chose the community playground as his haven. Numb from his reaction, she missed the approach of her groggy houseguest until Holt's shoulder nudged hers by the door.

"Something wrong?" He ran a hand through his hair but barely tamed the rumple.

"Mitch asked about Bicycle Man, so I laid out the truth and it didn't go over well."

"Go figure." He exhaled with exaggeration. "Guess I don't look much like a super hero right now. Maybe I can lure him back with some leftover Mexican food and lots of charm."

"Good luck with that." Her voice fell flat against the front door glass. Before Holt could refine his superhero effort, she turned away to go start a load of laundry.

~

Dinnertime sat with morbid somberness as Holt tried to regain the boy's admiration and assuage his fears. Not even macaroni and cheese with a hot dog partner could provide any support for his side of the tug-of-war across the table. Cami smiled between bites and did her best to engage Mitch in conversation, but one-syllable responses came as the minimum payoff. Holt wondered if the boy's nonacceptance clued something deeper, like objection to the suddenness of his appearance into their tight family unit. They needed a little more breathing room, so he decided to toss out an idea for group inspection.

He dusted potato chip crumbs off his palms. "Hey guys, I've been thinking about moving my things over to Joyce's side early, you know, to have my own space and all."

Cami's head snapped up, indicating her surprise at his suggestion, while Mitch kept chewing a mouthful of cheese-coated noodles. "You're welcome here, Holt, so don't think you aren't." She rested her fork on the placemat.

Holt took a long sip of water and hoped he didn't

seem ungrateful for all she had done so far. He looked at her over his glass rim and conveyed his earnest appreciation, albeit without words. Mitch's foot began tapping the chair leg under the table as he cleared his mouth to speak. Cami tried to squelch his comment with a stern look, but the boy shrugged it off.

"Here's another thing I don't understand. Why did you have your things already packed up when Mom went to get the bike at your apartment? It's like you were thinking of quitting already, even before the accident." Mitch stabbed the pile of macaroni and swirled his fork.

Holt's jaw dropped open, caught with his guard down without any answer that would make sense except the obvious one—that he had given up on everything— which he could never admit to such an impressionable boy.

"I've told you, Mitch." Cami balled her napkin in her fist. "Holt is not a quitter. Really, he's anything but…"

"Ha! That's not what Bo told me," the boy replied. "He said Holt was a weak link and we should get shed of him as soon as possible." He took a mouthful of noodles, seeming pleased with the rendering.

"When did you see Bo?" Her words came slow and pointed. "You weren't even here when he came to check Holt's hip."

"He stopped by the playground this afternoon." Mitch looked at her briefly and then picked up his hot dog. "I told him you said Holt was Bicycle Man and he laughed. Guess that makes two of us that don't believe your version."

"Bo doesn't have the time of day for the

homeless." Cami launched a defense, standing up for Holt by means of comparison. When Holt slid his chair back and stood, Cami's expression froze.

"Maybe I should be spending more time with Bo," Mitch added, "since we think alike and all." More macaroni disappeared into his mouth, a smug look on his face. A knock on the back glass was followed by the sliding door opening. Mitch looked over his shoulder. "Hey! Cookies for me…"

"For everyone." Joyce closed the door behind her. After one glance at Cami's embattled face, she halted. "What's going on in here?"

"I think I need to ask if I can move over to your side a couple of days early," Holt said in an attempt to diffuse the conflict. "My roommate and I seem to be having some issues over some misconceptions that I can clarify later."

Joyce tightened her lips, giving his sudden request some consideration. "If it would help restore balance on this half, then I think it's wise for you to shift over. And we could use the extra time to go over details like the fuse box and the water shutoff lever. As is customary before I leave town, I would like us all to plan for a family outing together tomorrow. Therefore, I'll make your early arrival conditional on Saturday's outing, if you think you could say yes."

Cami shot Holt a look that made his decision easier. "The family outing sounds fun, actually," he replied. "I'll pack my things and be over in half an hour, Joyce. I had plans to weed the patio flower beds this evening, but I might tackle that right now while the lighting's good."

"Very well then. Let me go move my suitcases off

your bed." Joyce uncovered the plate of cookies and left it on the table. Mitch leaned over and snagged a handful, but lost one to his mother's protective grip.

Holt sensed a battle waging on more fronts than the dessert platter as he dried his hands and left the kitchen. The sliding door opened and closed, followed by the hushed sound of Cami's cautionary warning to the boy, but he headed down the hall determined to mind his own business before more damage could be done. His reputation was in more shambles than his skin.

~

Smoldering at the table as her world spun out of control, Cami looked straight at her rebellious son. She had to respond to his latest testing of the boundaries she'd set. "Mitchell Lancaster Walsh, you listen to me and listen good. Holt Ellis is a God-fearing, talented man with a heart of gold. He's had some hard times, being unemployed, but that does not give you permission to call him things that he's not. And Holt is not a quitter. He wants to be Bicycle Man again. Maybe we could even help him find other ways to help the homeless once he comes back. Most of all, Holt is special to me. I expect you to treat him with respect, do you understand?"

"Then Holt's your friend and not mine. Bo's my friend," Mitch replied.

Cami clenched her teeth to keep from blurting out the truth, that high-and-mighty Bo had abandoned the boy from Day One. That choice bore no semblance of respect. Mitch left the table with globs of macaroni left behind. Some mess she'd gotten herself into now.

Chapter 10

Classical music intermixed with the aroma of chocolate chip cookies as Holt stepped through the sliding door into Joyce's side of the duplex. A sophisticated décor greeted him in shades of burgundy and gold, though no hostess appeared. He glanced around to evaluate his new surroundings as her humming grew louder from the hallway.

Joyce startled with a blink and tossed a hand towel onto the countertop. "So, what do you think?"

"Side A is totally different from side B and too fancy for the likes of me." He bent to lower his first box.

"No, no, no." She pointed over her shoulder. "Go right to your room and set up shop. Put your things where you want them. I tried to make some room for you in the closet by moving my winter wardrobe out."

"You're going to way too much trouble for me."

Holt hefted the box and lugged it toward the second bedroom. "I have two hang-up shirts and a rude assortment of worn-out T-shirts that aren't too proud to grace the back of a chair."

"I always encourage civility no matter the humble estate." She smiled as though to soften her expectation. "Life is what you make it, which reflects how you respect yourself and your own things."

Holt groaned as the box found the floor beside the neatly made twin bed. The furniture all matched and had a definite style, maybe Danish, sleek and ageless. "I only have one more box." He turned around to repeat the routine.

"No matter, bring it all. I need to clean up my baking mess in the kitchen. Maybe we can share an iced tea later and get caught up on the day's triumphs and woes."

"Tea sounds good, but my triumph tally might be on the short side." He ran his fingers through his hair as he passed her, headed for the sink, his thoughts swirling. Once out on the patio, he found that Cami had placed his second box outside her door with a post-it note on top. With a deep breath, he flattened the note and glanced at the one-liner.

"Sweet of you to give us space," he read. "Time heals all wounds to lend its grace." He tucked the heart message into his T-shirt pocket and retrieved the box, his material tether to the planet. As uncomfortable as this interim seemed, at least he could heal and find a direction.

~

Cami tugged spaceship pajamas down her son's still-wet back. "What if you could wave a magic wand

and slay a bad guy with one hand?"

Mitch shook his moptop like a dog. "If that's all it took, then why wouldn't I do it?" The cat ran out of the bathroom in objection to the wet treatment.

Caution was in order here, as they approached a serious subject matter. She wanted to keep it light. She looked at his reflection in the mirror and locked her gaze on his face. "You might get your chance tomorrow, so I wanted to ask you about it first. The clinic wants us to donate some DNA for their records. They'll keep it for identification purposes. Part of that is to show that you're my son, as our DNA is more alike than anyone else in the whole world. That makes us family."

The boy threw an arm around her neck, releasing a whiff of action hero bubble bath. "Does this mean I have to give blood? Man, I hate getting poked like that." His mouth scrunched to the side to reflect his displeasure.

"No, sweetie. No needles and no poking this time, thank goodness." She grabbed his comb and swept his thick brown hair to the side. "The magic wand is really a cotton swab and they swish it across the inside of our cheeks. It catches enough cells that they sample our DNA from it and we're done, just like that."

"Then where does slaying the bad guy come in?" He backed away, out of her grip.

Cami had to give this some thought, as there was no bad guy threatening them, only circumstance. She picked his dirty clothes up and fished for a wayward sock. "Well, I guess we don't know who the bad guy is right now, honey. But if one ever surfaces, we'll have our DNA work already done."

She would not disclose the current problem at the clinic, or the ugly truth that would emerge once she sat down to fill out her testimony form. Most likely a villain would surface as the investigation proceeded, but Mitch could be spared the brunt of that revelation. Only the guilty dog would have to face up to his behavior. The innocent would remain free from any guilt-association. Yes, it had been a long time coming, but she was finally committed to it.

"Can I watch Animal Planet until bedtime?" Mitch ran toward the living room with his favorite stuffed animal hunkered in his clutches.

A swinging option for Friday night, she'd spend it as a mother hen hovering over a den full of monkeys. "Okay, I guess," she replied with a sigh. "I'll do my paperwork in the dining room."

~

Holt lowered his tea glass and caught Joyce's direct stare.

"Are you ready to tell me what kind of wrecking ball hit the three of you next door?"

He couldn't hide his astonishment at her clairvoyance. In all fairness, he couldn't think of an appropriate starting point, as they all seemed to condemn him. "The crux of the matter is that Mitchell thinks I'm a quitter because, as a community servant, I left the homeless to fend for themselves. I've fallen from grace in his eyes and it's driving a wedge between mother and son." He tried yawning to control his nervousness but it failed to work.

"You were involved with charity work before the accident?"

"Yes. I don't know if you've been following the

newspaper's story of Bicycle Man."

Her eyes danced with mirth. "You, Holt Ellis, are Bicycle Man?"

"Scratched up and marred on the surface, but underneath, I'm Bicycle Man. The crazy thing is, the boy's right, in a way. I probably am a quitter, but not in the way he thinks."

"How so then? How are you giving up?"

He stretched his legs out under the coffee table only to shrink back in a cringe. "That particular trip up the mountain was not an accident, a recreational outing, or a joy ride. I planned it after I couldn't think of another way out."

"Out of..."

"Long-term unemployment, depression probably, starvation definitely—a combination of failures had pushed me to the far edge of desperation. The funny thing was, though, I never lost my faith in all of it. I tried to look for the lessons, tried to have perseverance through the struggle, but somehow hard circumstances never let up. Even that day on top of the mountain, I prayed and thanked God for his provision. Then I relinquished my portion. Guess that capped my ride as a quitter's recourse. Lastly, I prayed for his will to be done as I made the trip down to desperation's intersection at the bottom of the mountain."

"What exactly was supposed to happen at that juncture?" Joyce traced the rim of her glass with her fingertip without looking up.

"A horrible accident might occur, one where a speeding cyclist would have little hope to survive," he replied. His chin dropped as he wrestled with the truth. In hindsight, it would have been a hard finale to pull off.

Joyce made a noise in her throat. "Instead, God's will was done. Cami intervened midway into this desperate plan. Does she know the truth about the setup?"

"I've talked to her about not having hope in my situation. I told her I needed her, and that part is truthful. My whole life changed the instant we met, and as painful as it has been for me to come back, I relish every step. I gave it to God up on that mountaintop, and I believe he brought us together in his divine will. I've seen what a full life can be like now. I love her, Joyce."

"But I believe there's a spiritual step missing here, despite your heartfelt contrition and your positive turnaround." Her tone seemed cautionary.

Holt glanced up, confused but open to guidance. Hairs began to stand up on his forearms. For the life of him, he couldn't think of anything he'd left out. He shook his head when words wouldn't come.

"You gave up your portion up there, remember? And now you've had a glimpse of what kind of blessing God has in store for you, so you want it back, if I'm not mistaken."

He blew out a breath as his mind filled with stories from the Bible where blessings had been withheld. Those stories never painted a pretty outcome.

"Yes, I want my portion reinstated." He spoke the words with conviction as though staking a claim. "I want every last blessing God intends for me. And I don't want to mess up anyone else's allotment, either." Moisture drained from his mouth. The sensation to throw up struck right then and there. Out of alignment with the Almighty God—it scared him to death.

Joyce crossed her ankles. "Begging might not be inappropriate from your position of… disenfranchisement, Holt. You need to have a heart-to-heart talk with God and set matters straight. Then your relationships with Cami and Mitchell will find a way to work out. Why don't you grab a hot shower before you retire? I've left a Bible on your nightstand, in case you find the urge to seek some time-proven answers to life's many questions."

He stood and pulled at his shirttail, out of sorts with himself. "Thank you, Joyce, for your candor and for pointing me back toward God, a logical direction."

"You're most welcome. As for me, I'm going to finish packing before bedtime. A special friend called and requested that I arrive a few days early. Given the situation here, I think that's the right course of action."

He managed a faint nod. Now he had to unknot his own hitch, hot water notwithstanding.

~

Clawed from the inside out, Cami forced her hand to write on the testimony form. The first blanks held minor information—dates, times, and parties involved. She looked at Bo's name after printing it out and tried to dodge the hurt. Now she had arrived at the testimony portion of the page where blank lines begged for sequential details of the event. How could she release herself to think about that horrible day after so many years of blocking it out?

Her thoughts drifted to Lyric Baldwin, the sweet girl who had done nothing to draw herself into a conundrum but fall down a mountain. What could Cami have done to protect her? Maybe stay by her side, only that didn't follow protocol for the clinic where staff seemed constantly stretched thin. The nurses did the setup and the doctors followed up with the diagnosis. The system wasn't flawed, the staff was—one staff member in particular. The look on Lyric's face as she ran out of the clinic flashed to mind, her wound fresh from being approached out of the blue.

Her pen found the page again, stop-and-start at first, but gaining fluidity as she recounted the setting and how she came to be alone that fateful day. The first-year nursing practicum scores were due to be posted, but there had been a last-minute change. Doctor Ballard claimed the nursing supervisor had asked him to give the evaluations and he chose to release them one by one in private sessions. Yes, she would record the exchange as innocently as it had started out, then take it through to its life-shattering end. She owed that to Lyric, but more importantly, she owed it to herself.

The television droned on about the protracted gestation of an elephant as she found herself transported back to that examination room. After hours, the doors were locked. The doctor perched on a stool at the built-in desk with his review of her work spread on the countertop. His reception had been warm as she entered the room. Cami couldn't remember if she had smiled back or not, nervous for her grades. After focusing her attention on the line items of individual scores he indicated, she felt the first trespass—his arm around her shoulders. Mistaken for support, she withheld her initial objection at the contact. He made a suggestive joke in an attempt to loosen her up. By the bottom of the score sheet, she'd be in for a rude awakening. Somehow they weren't talking about her grades anymore.

Bo offered to give her special attention to ensure

she made the cut. His voice had turned husky as he enjoyed her proximity, much more than she appreciated his. In fact, she thought to run away and end the ordeal more than once. Instead, she planted herself beside him to finish the review. She wanted to receive his evaluation so she could benefit from the feedback before the second year of the nursing program began. She had given it her best effort, but it nagged at her that she hadn't heard of any other students getting such personal attention.

Suddenly, his expression turned wild and his hands began to trespass everywhere. He pushed her against the examination table and trapped her verbal protests with his mouth. He proceeded with purposeful mal-intent. She fell victim to his attack, without consent and without provocation. That's when the hush-up began.

Cami forced her hand to record the details for the first time in eight years. Her left hand smeared the tears on her cheeks as her right hand wrote out the reason. She didn't stop until the last detail came to mind. Bo laughed and told her she had passed with flying colors. The final knife stab took her breath away.

Mitch stretched in the doorway. "I'm heading for bed now. Come say my prayers?"

She dried her cheeks and smiled up at him. "Of course I will, sweetie. We always need to talk to God, don't we?"

~

Holt trudged toward the shower with a pair of gym shorts in his hands. Something about having a broken and contrite heart seemed too simple. Esau had sold his birthright to Jacob the schemer just to gain a bowl of beans. Hadn't he meant the opposite when he'd prayed from the mountaintop that day? He'd wanted God to give his provision to someone else, as he didn't think he needed it anymore. Now he hungered for something that seemed out of his grasp and beyond his control. Longing for Cami rose in his chest and he closed the bathroom door. He braced against it as if to hold the attraction at bay.

Holt shirked off his shirt and slung it into the corner by the tub. *How could love have so much power?* He glanced at his image in the mirror. Still repulsive, though his scrapes vanished daily and his split lip had healed by increments. The sinewy gauntness of his profile had given way to fuller proportions. He still needed a haircut. Maybe he could ask Joyce to do the honors in the morning. A deeper ugliness lurked in his eyes, dark and haunting.

He bent and turned the water faucet on full blast, then backed it off to a steady spray. He shucked off the remainder of his clothes. Somehow the prayer came. As he stepped in, the steam helped him open up. He wanted his portion back and he would downright beg for it if that's what God required. He began to voice his protest loud and clear.

~

How she forgot to put this last load in the dryer, Cami couldn't imagine. The hour late, she stood bone weary and emotionally spent. Still, Mitch needed his gym clothes for PE Monday so she went through the motions to finish the cycle. She threw the last fistful of wet fabric into the dryer's tub, cleared the filter, and pressed the start button. A moan followed, but the drum began to turn. The red light assured her the appliance worked. When the moan repeated, it sounded more human in origin, not mechanical.

Then Holt's distinct voice penetrated the laundry room wall with chanted repetition. His audible admission to God melted right through her exhaustion. Her knees buckled and deposited her onto the floor beside the mop. She tucked her head as he called for his portion in a desperate overture. When her name became mixed in the word-flurry, she began to weep until every wounded ounce leaked out.

Chapter 11

She could not have been more stunned. Cami let Holt in the sliding door and there he stood, complete with a stylish haircut. His ironed shirt lent him a professional appearance. He'd never looked better. Her heart thumped inside her chest. She had to look away before she betrayed her feelings.

Holt flashed a pleasant smile as though he truly anticipated spending quality time with them today. "How are you this morning?" He dipped down to catch her gaze.

"I, uh, I'm fine. I had a productive night coming to terms with a few loose ends. I hope Joyce told you that we need to go by the clinic after lunch."

"Yeah, she mentioned it, but we don't have to let it mar the rest of the day." He turned to search for something. "Joyce has decided to leave after church tomorrow. Said a friend in Maine wants her there early, so she's giving me the run of the place. I hope that works out well for everyone."

Cami squelched her protest at being the last to know Joyce's change of plans, as Mitch had just walked into the room. She intended this to remain a positive day.

"Morning, Mitch."

"Hey, Holt. How'd you like being on the other side?"

"I'm walking around with my hands in my pockets trying not to break any of Joyce's nice stuff." His tone had a tease to it. "Other than that, what's not to like? I have a room to myself in a house that smells like cookies."

Cami rewarded him with a smirk-turned-smile for relating things at kid level. Aunt Joyce appeared at the back door and Holt slid it open to let her in.

"Are we all set?" Joyce inspected the crew as her purse swung on her arm. "We'll take Cami's car."

"I'll sit in back with Mitch," Holt said.

Joyce put up a hand of protest. "That's my spot beside Mitchell, as this is typically our day as a twosome. We're just letting you and Cami tag along to give you something constructive to do with your time."

Holt had an impish gleam in his eye. "Oh, is that the way it is?"

Cami stepped by him with a quick wink and pressed Mitch toward the door.

"Okay. Guess I'll ride up front with the other pretty lady, then." Holt shrugged his shoulders and buried his hands in his pockets.

Joyce gave him a teasing smile as she passed. "Funny how I usually get what I want."

"Can you teach me how to do that?" Holt asked as he followed along. With a shove of the door and a turn of the key, the play day gained traction.

Cami's trip meter only registered four miles when Aunt Joyce directed her to turn off Highway 6 into an industrial park. The metal buildings clustered around an unlined parking lot didn't exactly exude interest at first glance. Once she'd stepped through the doorway of the oversized warehouse, she readily changed her mind. "Ooh, what is this place?"

Soft lighting settled like dust around rows and rows of crated rock samples while more ornate specimens sat on pallets out in the open. Holt walked past her and introduced himself to a slab of copper ore that looked like a flattened meteorite—bronzed metallic in color, and polished to eye-popping perfection.

"Thirty-five thousand." Mitch tapped the small sticker along its edge.

"I can't take my eyes off this thing," Holt replied, mesmerized by the slab.

Cami laughed, nudged his shoulder, and soon found a row of shaped stone interesting. She selected a milky pink heart and flashed it in his direction.

"Make yourself look down every aisle, or you'll miss something even more spectacular." Joyce searched down a deep row that reached the rear of the warehouse. "Mitchell, let's see if we can find our buddy Chris. He's probably cutting something in back with the wet saw." The boy ran off like he'd found familiar territory.

Cami shrugged her shoulders and traced an arching dolphin carved from a lustrous gray stone that seemed to glitter inside.

"Labradorite," Joyce said. "It has fire inside, like an opal—a dark blue flame."

Holt pointed to the center of the warehouse where a series of oversized shipping crates sat aligned. "Let's go find out what's in those bins over there."

With reluctance, Cami left the carved stone table and followed her entourage into the storage caverns ahead. She stopped at the first crate and peered over the chest-high side. Holt joined her, leaning against her side. The rock samples inside cast a spell over them.

"Holy rockslide, Batman." Holt gave a low whistle and reached in to touch the closest specimen.

Cami examined the block print on the crate, trying to trace its origin. "This one's from Morocco." She placed both hands over the side and picked up a chunk of milky green rock as slick as glass.

"That's chrysoprase," a man said from behind. "It's one of my particular favorites."

"Chris, this is my niece, Cami, and her friend, Holt." Joyce gestured with her introductions. "Everyone, please meet the brains and hands behind Stone Traders, Chris Markum."

"Quite a place you have here, Chris," Holt said, his face animated.

"Yeah, we're bringing in rough-cut rocks from all around the world," he replied. "My big boss travels to select and buy while I hold down the fort back here in Golden."

"You are being way too modest, Chris," Joyce said. "Under your skillful hands, the rough nuggets become works of art for commoners like us to treasure."

Cami examined the remainder of the bin, a tumble of color variation and texture. She discovered a jagged chunk of green mixed with purple and adored it with her fingertips.

"Fluorite," Chris offered. "Nature's most beautiful blend of colors, for sure, banded together. Ah, you might be interested to know where Mitch is while we're enjoying the big stuff."

So overwhelmed with the rock stash that she'd forgotten about her son, Cami gave the man a fear-filled look in response.

The rock smith held his hand up to reassure her all was well. "Follow me, please."

While Holt tucked a smile into his unscratched cheek, she became the guide's shadow to reunite with her son. When she saw what the boy had been doing, she was shocked. "Mitch, honey, do you have Mr. Markum's permission to be digging around in there?" This whole collection looked expensive and she didn't have an extra dime to spend on something inert like a fancy rock.

The boy looked up, guiltless, as his hands roamed about a large wooden crate. "No worries, Mom. Welcome to the official trash rock bin. If Mr. Chris messes up or the rock sample crumbles when he cuts it, it winds up in here."

"Take as much as you want," Chris said, "as it will only be thrown out."

Cami's lips tightened into a circle as the pile in front of the boy grew by another fist-sized rock. His newest was covered with spikes of crumbly crystals. Holt stooped to join the priceless adventure and scooped up a sample to give her, the same type of stone she'd been admiring back at the crate from Morocco.

"Chrysoprase," she said, this time expressed with

awe. The milky green chunk bubbled around a white frothy covering of teeny crystals.

"Crystalline gypsum-wrapped chrysoprase," Chris added. "I couldn't do anything with that small a specimen. It's all yours to have, if you like it."

She clutched it to her chest. "It's going from the trash straight to the treasure table." She gazed at Holt, his admiration unmistakable. Their relationship could be symbolized by a rock such as this, two individuals thrown away by society finding value in each other. She soon felt his arm wrap around her waist and the tickle of his lips on her earlobe.

"Your beauty beats all of these," he whispered.

Cami blushed in an emotional mix like the banded fluorite, another crystalline work of God's creative hand.

"You'll need a box for that load, Mitch." Chris stepped off to retrieve a carrying case for the new rock collection.

When he returned, Cami gasped at his choice, a satin-embossed oriental hinged box with a fancy latch on the front.

"This came in with our last shipment from China, but we don't have any purpose for this type of container." Chris twisted the box around toward Mitch.

The boy looked up and his jaw dropped at the exotic offering.

Joyce placed a hand on his shoulder, her face beaming. "What do you say, Mitchell?"

"Thanks a quadrillion, Chris." Mitch stood and dusted his hands off before accepting the generous gift.

Cami covered her mouth to keep from exclaiming, as the bric-a-brac collection became a true treasure trove in the beautiful box. She allowed the generosity of the moment to elevate her spirits. "How can we thank you enough?" She extended her free hand in gratitude.

"Thanks for keeping me company today, as it gets to be a pretty solitary existence out here," Chris replied. He pumped her hand and turned toward Holt.

An intense look swept over her date's face, a look that could usher in something unexpected, like a well-meaning complication. She clutched her rock in both hands.

Joyce pivoted toward the back of the building. "And now it's time for my special purchase of the day." Mitch hurried to fill the box with his final picks and stood beside her, determined not to be left out of that portion of the adventure. "Good, Mitch, you're with me."

Cami arched her eyebrows. What could the rest of the place be hiding?

Holt pointed a solitary finger in the air and held it there with expectation. "Chris, can I have a word with you for a minute?"

"Sure thing." The warehouse manager nodded toward his office and the two men departed.

Magnetically drawn to shadow her aunt, Cami wandered back through the rows of crates and samples into the valley of vast mineral selection.

~

Holt hoped to stage a platform for his next leap of faith. "This looks like a pretty low-key operation here at the warehouse."

"It's a low-key and low-budget operation, as we make our profit by selling to distributors all over the country who then sell to the public," Chris replied. His eye held a glint of receptivity.

Holt wanted to lead with the broad proposal and see which parts of his suggestion could survive closer scrutiny. "Bear with me a minute as I try to get the right perspective." He scanned the enormous warehouse for potential. Finally, he spotted a break room equipped with a microwave and a snack machine beyond a major backload of unrefined rock. "See, I work with the homeless in downtown Golden, mostly food distribution."

"Oh my word, you're not that Bicycle Man that's gone missing?" Chris studied his scraped exterior.

Holt gave a faint nod and a rush of courage filled his chest. He cleared his throat and began to brainstorm with his newfound associate. "These individuals need something to do with their hands—something constructive."

"Like sorting rock piles," Chris guessed.

A smile pulled against his split lip as Holt sensed the conversation lift out of the rock quarry and gain momentum. "I mean, a couple of these guys, Tom and Leroy, could be nightclub bouncers, they're so well built. And another fellow, Donnie, has the keenest eye for detail you can imagine."

"Like a sample packer would need."

"Or even a night watchman, whatever your need would pinpoint. On the surface, I see that you, the skill guy, have to do everything in this operation—from hauling in rough boulders to crating the finished product. Now if we could get you some help, and possibly even get someone to underwrite it with a grant, then it's a win-win for the community."

"Man, that sounds good to me. Beyond good,

actually." Chris rubbed his palms together. "We had contemplated getting some college kids from the School of Mines, but the big boss isn't fond of that age group because they typically lack proper motivation."

"I don't think you'd have to worry about that with these veterans. Listen, let me talk this arrangement around with the guys and give you a chance to run it by the big boss. Make sure he knows that it wouldn't have to involve an hourly wage. We could set up a stipend amount, maybe a credit line at Save Always for groceries. Something that would foster their independence and give them some pride back."

"I like the sound of this cooperative more and more," Chris replied. "We'd like to throw in a free lunch, just so you know up front. It's the least we could do for gaining some help around here."

Instinctively, he offered his hand and Chris took it, shaking with enthusiasm. Holt's voice turned gravelly as the idea settled on him. He tried to think ahead. "What would you expect in the way of training?"

"All on-the-job training, as I'd want to show them how myself."

Holt sensed the momentum of the new project and wanted to ride it for all it was worth. "Mind if I ask what you were trained in to have such expertise cutting the stone?"

Chris laughed and crossed his arms over his chest. "My training? I was a dental hygienist before I came here. It's much the same if you look at the parallels. Wet cleanup work on hard surfaces in fairly tight confines."

"Well, you sure landed in the right place." Holt held out his arms to mimic the expanse of opportunity awaiting them. A pleasurable yelp from the back aisle reminded him that a special purchase might have been landed.

Already ahead of him, Chris charged past the front desk to reconnect with his customers. He stopped for a moment and slid something off the desk, then turned and handed a business card to Holt. "Call me next week and let's try to get this off the ground." He hastened down the length of the warehouse and disappeared.

Holt pocketed the little slip of hope and knew he had connected two highly needy parties, if both would cooperate. He broke into a jog to find the shoppers.

Joyce pointed to the back shelf. "This is what we want."

Holt looked over Cami's shoulder at the dimly lit shelf. A row of block-carved nightlights stood in a line and illuminated at Chris's touch as he worked switches on down the way. One by one, pillars of crystal transformed to columns of light from a single bulb at each color-filled base. The glow created the most beautiful aurora on the back wall.

Chris returned to the group. "This is an interesting combination we've had lots of success with. It's a clear gypsum column that gives the light its height, and that's fitted into a colorful base of fluorite."

Joyce shifted Mitch's shoulders straight with the display. "Now you get to pick which one you want."

Holt rested his hands on Cami's shoulders to share her delight in the moment.

Mitch toed down the line until he paused at a particularly colorful combination, with a purple band cutting a swath through the green base.

Joyce stepped back with a look of satisfaction on

her face. "Let Chris get it out for us, sweetheart."

"You bet. These weigh more than what you might think." Chris unplugged and pulled the boy's selection off the shelf. With it cradled in both hands, he walked them to the front.

"Well, that's why we brought Holt along with us, to carry all our purchases," Joyce replied.

Holt gave her a wink. "It's nice to be needed." His tone teased but he fully meant it. Cami's arm slid through his elbow and he locked it down against his rejuvenating core, the salvaged rock tucked between them for good measure. He ventured a glance at her face and received what he wanted, a mineral deposit of the magnetic kind.

Chapter 12

Golden's Pioneer Museum smelled like an interesting mix of old books and furniture polish. Cami amused herself with their postcard collection while she waited for the tour to start. Two other families had signed in for the same tour time and were milling about the lobby. Holt had taken Mitch to the men's room and Aunt Joyce conversed with the clerk behind the gift shop register. She glanced at her watch, knowing the one-thirty appointment at the clinic wouldn't budge. All other involvements were relegated to filler status.

The tinkle of a small bell sounded across the room and Cami glanced up to see Holt threading his way back through the gift shop toward her. Aunt Joyce broke off her conversation and turned, so she waved to get her attention. A docent placed the bell back by the register and took a position to greet her tour group.

Mitch slammed Cami with a running hug that caused her to lose her balance, but Holt came up on the other side to steady her.

"We're so honored to have you with us today," the docent said. "Whether you're from close by or far away, we trust you will learn something new about the pioneers who traveled through the Rockies and settled this area. I'm Lily, your humble guide. I'll point out some things our forefathers left us from their trail blazing days. Without further ado, let's enjoy the collection together."

Joyce reached for Mitch's hand and Cami relinquished possession of the boy.

Holt brushed her arm with his. "Is this hand taken?"

She shushed him with a coy smile and moved toward him. The quiet imposed by the museum held a magnetic quality. They passed by the restricting railing and entered a small collection of pre-electronic gadgets, including an antique crank record player, its oak cabinet restored to mint condition. Mitch reached out to touch a hooded camera atop a tripod, which must have cued the docent into action.

"Now here's a word of advice to help our museum stay nice," she quoted in singsong simplicity. "If you keep your hands to yourself, the treasures keep longer on their shelf! I know it's so hard not to touch sometimes, but looking is a form of admiration, too. And I'll make a deal with you, young man. I'll need an assistant later on to handle some of our display pieces, and I'll pick you—if you're being good."

Mitch nodded his cooperation as Aunt Joyce bent down to whisper an encouragement in his ear. Cami realized that they were both helping her shape her son into a better human being, and she took comfort in the thought.

Holt nodded toward the camera cache and she shifted her attention to its offering. "I'd like to have a photo of you," he whispered, his eyes intense.

Cami cleared her throat and moved him forward with a tiny push, deciding not to respond. She didn't have a recent picture anyway, unless one of the candid shots Aunt Joyce was always taking with her phone counted.

"I'm truly flattered," she replied in a low voice. "But can we wait until my bangs grow out?" She watched a confused look surface on his face as the group rounded the bend toward a gold-mining exhibit. He leaned forward with a comeback and she braced herself for teasing in front of a sepia panorama featuring a mule team.

"You're jealous of my haircut, aren't you?" Mirth danced in his eyes.

Cami heard a metallic click as she laughed out loud and Aunt Joyce lowered her phone, moving a finger to her lips. Now she had been captured with her museum companion for posterity. Trapped in the moment, she felt like part of the mining display, only not as old.

~

Holt mentally traced what remained of their circuitous route from the piano burial place back to the open lobby and knew the tour had to be near its end. The docent droned on about how the pioneers were so fond of music as part of their cultural preservation, they were willing to haul these weighty pianos in covered wagons over hill and vale. The mountains, however, presented a more formidable barrier and many a load had to be lightened before that crossing could be accomplished. She positioned the group in front of a most unique upright model, covered in crushed velvet, a color that he could only interpret as an ugly burnt orange.

"This is one piece that we allow our patrons to touch," Lily said. "Does anyone play?" She glanced at a delicate young girl dressed in a lace skirt, but she shook her braid-capped head. Mitch took a step forward, which made Cami stiffen. When Joyce nodded and smiled, the boy slid onto the bench and studied the keys. One mellow note at a time, a classic German piece emanated from the instrument, all played to perfection from memory. Moved, the docent clasped her hands under her chin to keep it from quivering. Several of the women looked tearful when the song concluded, including the two with which Holt had arrived.

"Well," the docent said, stopping to swallow. "That was the timeless 'Fur Elise' for those who didn't recognize it, and I do believe this old piano just came to life for the sheer benefit of those of us in the room. This is what makes history so relevant, as we are connected to those who came before us, because they shared many of the same likes and dislikes, could be moved by the same music that now moves us, and had hope for the same tomorrow that keeps our hearts stirred for what comes next. Bravo, young man."

"What a beautiful end to our tour, Lily," Holt replied in genuine appreciation. Joyce began a round of applause as Cami wrapped the pianist in a hug. The lacey little girl stepped forward and offered Mitch a candy stick which immediately turned the maestro back into a fourth grade goofball. Holt's heart stirred with something akin to parental pride. What covered wagon *that* had ridden in on he had no idea.

~

Cami glanced at her watch again. "We'll have to do a hurry-up lunch. I'm sorry, Aunt Joyce. I know you would have liked something nicer." A breeze blew off the river as they stood by the car trying to decide where to go next.

"Nonsense, Cami," she replied. "I have favorites in every category, and a toasted sandwich at Subterranean would suit me just fine. Holt, how about you? Would a sub sandwich hit the spot?"

He tossed a sheepish look at Cami. "Sure, I like just about everything but anchovies. It looks like Mitch wants cheese melted all over a big sub roll, plus whatever meat comes with it."

The boy smiled ear-to-ear. "A cold-cut combo."

"My all-time favorite, too," Holt replied. "With mustard or mayo?"

"Both!" Mitch held up his palm and the two exchanged a high five in celebration of their culinary collusion.

Cami pulled at both of them. "Don't forget we're in a bit of a hurry, gentlemen."

"Well, I think we just made your order a little easier, since we can share a mile-high sandwich together," Holt replied.

Joyce led them across the street toward the deli where they were seated in record time.

"One mile-high cold-cut combo, hold the peppers, and one mile-high roasted chicken with Vidalia onion sauce, peppers on the side, plus a basket of chips," Cami said. "We're watching the clock today, so quick is good."

"Got it," the young waitress replied. She disappeared with the order as if to prove it.

Holt stood. "Come on, maestro, let's go wash that piano off your hands." He clapped his hands together. Cami pecked the boy's cheek as reward for his musical gift to the tour group.

"Aw shucks." Mitch pinched his cheek to form a dimple.

"Man," Holt exclaimed. "Now I'm going to have to learn how to play the piano so the chicks can dig me like that."

Joyce gave him a patronizing pat on the arm.

Cami excused them with a wry nod and waited for them to head out of hearing distance. "I'm starting to get a little nervous about the clinic meeting." She fingered the napkin.

Joyce reached over and encircled her wrist with her fingers as though to take her pulse. "Today we put an end to this travesty," she said, her gaze rock solid.

"Let's try to leave enough time after lunch to check back by the duplex, as I'd rather go in with a full load of ammo. Lyric's testimony should come in today's mail."

"As hungry as I am, eating fast shouldn't be a problem. What will we do with Holt? Do we bring him along as an outside party?"

Cami hesitated while the server placed the chip basket on the table. "No, he wants to go down to Clear Creek. He's already cooking up a work co-op for the homeless with Chris at the rock shop, believe it or not."

Her lunch companion smiled and placed her napkin in her lap with delicate precision. She popped a dollop of anti-bacterial hand sanitizer onto her palms and passed the bottle to Cami for her use. "Oh, I believe it to be true. That Holt is a networker extraordinaire, especially if it includes being charitable in any way."

Cami saw the guys approaching from the back hall. "That's a good thing, right?"

"That's a God-given thing." Joyce's face animated as she greeted her guests with a smile.

Cami relaxed to enjoy their amicable lunch, the calm before the storm. She had called forth this storm to end the tempest that had beset her for so long. Time to let it rain.

~

Holt stood on the flat rock near the bridge and held the sandwich bags up until the familiar signal got him the attention he desired. That instant held his reward for requesting the improperly made sandwiches from the call-in order at Subterranean. He hadn't planned to bait the work initiative, but he had to appeal to their basic needs first. A fundamental rule in working with the homeless, he thought he had memorized it.

Leroy wandered out of the shade first, tossing his familiar two-fingered wave. Lucy followed three steps behind, slow paced but every bit as interested. Holt bid his time by praying silently that there would be some positive interest in his idea. As his words sailed upward, he realized that God could make anything possible. So why should he hesitate to put it out there?

Leroy reached for the closest bag. "I wasn't expecting you on the weekend, Bicycle Man."

Holt pulled the bag away to give the old woman a

chance to catch up.

"Who wants ham and who wants salami?"

"Ham for me." Lucy raised her free hand to accept it. Holt released it into her custody and surrendered the second bag to Leroy.

"I have something I want to talk to you both about." Holt held his arms up. "I have a friend who needs some help at a warehouse that specializes in rock collections. Big chunks of rocks come in from all over the world, beautiful rough chips and boulders of every kind of stone you can imagine."

"What does that matter to us?" Leroy shifted, his tone impatient. Lucy tapped her walking stick on the rock as if to prompt him.

Holt began to second-guess himself about the perfect match thing he had conceptualized. "Well, the guy who cuts the rock down and puts it into smaller collections with other rocks is doing everything right now, from the time the rocks come in until they ship out. He really needs some help. I'm willing to set up a work arrangement for you guys, but only if you're willing to pitch in with an honest day's work."

"I've always been a bit of a rock hound." Leroy rolled the top of the sandwich bag in his hands. "That kind of job would be like throwing me back into the briar patch, Bicycle Man. But what about wheels? Could you find some way for me to get out there?"

"That's one of the aspects I'd have to work out, maybe line up a transit bus pass or something."

"The Senior Center has a van for making such runs around the area," Lucy added.

"Another good possibility," Holt gave her his undivided attention. "How does work sound to you,

Miss Lucy?"

"What kind of pay you talkin' about?"

"How about a food account at Save Always with your name on it?"

"Count me in and let me know when to start." Leroy stepped away with his sandwich.

Lucy turned to follow and was nearly under the bridge before she gave him her reply. "Make it two of us, only I ain't picking up no heavy rocks. I can dust and clean though, and I bet he hadn't done that in forever."

Holt laughed at her insight, as she was spot-on with her supposition. That made him two-for-two at his first stop. Now he had to go win a game of checkers up higher on the creek.

~

Cami wheeled the car into Valley Vista and made a beeline toward her mailbox while Joyce reapplied her lipstick. She glimpsed Mitch in her rearview mirror, playing with the rock fragments in his treasure chest. As they passed the playground, she spotted something familiar out of the corner of her eye.

"Don't look up," she whispered to Joyce, who continued her touch-up in the vanity mirror on her visor. "Let's just get this and go." She pulled into the drive far enough to open the mailbox flap and extracted the mail. She handed it to her aunt, shifted into reverse, and began to backtrack out of the neighborhood. This time, she scanned the playground parking lot as they sped by.

"BMW?" Joyce mouthed to her. "What's he doing here?" Her question came laced with suspicion.

"S-t-a-l-k-i-n-g," she replied under her breath. The

two exchanged glances as Joyce fanned out the mail for her inspection. There it was, second to the left. Lyric had followed through and now, together, they would be a force to be reckoned with. Keeping a furtive watch in the rearview mirror, Cami turned toward the medical clinic for her appointment with the board of directors' legal advisor. In less than a mile, she would have justice—if only she could breath. She glanced at her speedometer and considered her tenuous position. She was simply being an ordinary, law-abiding citizen. Then why the white-knuckled ride?

Chapter 13

Cami stood by the conference room table. "Dr. Harrison, thank you for being willing to come in on Saturday."

Joyce reappeared from the hallway, having successfully situated Mitch in a small waiting room just outside with his hand-held game.

Two men sat on the far side of the table, both with stern expressions until a ray of lightheartedness rode a shoulder shrug. "My golf game will have to wait one more week to improve." He opened the folder in front of him. "Let me make introductions first off. Ladies, this is Aaron Stallings, the board's legal counsel and a district judge. Mr. Stallings, this is one of my best nurses, Cami Walsh, and her aunt, Joyce Lancaster."

Mr. Stallings stood to shake hands. "My pleasure." He indicated for the women to be seated.

Cami took the closest chair and felt uncomfortable

right away. The impulse to burst out of the room and run from the ugly truth started in her trembling knees and vibrated up her backbone, but she held her place. Joyce adjusted her chair to face the legal counsel directly and held herself with regal ease, which caused Cami to straighten in her seat. The first pulse of confidence trickled through her veins.

"Let me start out by requesting the written accounts from the victims of the alleged sexual battery." Judge Stallings' words echoed around the otherwise empty room with authority.

Cami produced two envelopes for him, Lyric's sealed letter and her own testimony. Doctor Harrison reached across the table with a slight smile and received the evidence that would get the ball of justice rolling.

"While we study these, let me provide you with a summary of the history of prosecution for this type of crime." The judge produced a single typed page. Doctor Harrison again served as the go-between. Joyce nodded her appreciation as she drew the sheet between them to read together.

Cami hesitated, but a confident look from Joyce inspired her to look the devil in the eye. One of the catchphrases of nursing school had been "Knowledge replaces fear." She couldn't feign ignorance at this point, so she made herself read the summary. By the end of the first paragraph that highlighted the victim's typical reluctance to step forward, the familiar taste of passive guilt filled the back of her throat. She was the poster child of failure to prosecute, or had been, up until today.

Somewhere within the contents of the second paragraph, Cami found her footing and became heartened by the status of the law protecting the innocent, as well as the success of cases that had been brought to court. For the first time, she could actually conceive a victory in this area where before she had settled for defeat. A release of inhibition came with the thought, and she looked up at her aunt with the determination she had been lacking. Joyce found her hand and gave it a squeeze. Cami knew she should take the lead from here on in. She was more than ready.

The men switched testimony papers and for the first time, Cami wondered what Lyric had written and whether it would be condemning enough. She reflected on her own detailed account and felt momentarily exposed. A silent prayer went up and the Holy Spirit fortified her from within. Doctor Harrison cleared his throat nervously and Cami glanced up, recognizing her own handwriting through the paper. She braced for their interrogation and whatever else might come with it.

Finally, both men finished their review. The judge collected the papers and tucked them into the pocket of his folder. "It is my opinion that we have enough testimony to launch an investigation into these allegations that will become the core of our case against Doctor Ballard. Several matters need to be addressed next. I hope we can count on your full cooperation, Ms. Walsh."

Cami exhaled with newfound freedom as Joyce patted her hand again under the table. When Mitch spoke out from his game-playing perch in the hall, Cami remembered her only hesitation.

"Count on me, Judge Stallings," she said in a low voice, "but I'd like to screen Mitchell from the damaging truth as much as possible. He doesn't know that Bo Ballard is his biological father and I have no intention of telling him at this time. Doctor Ballard made it crystal clear from the day Mitchell was born that he would not have any involvement with either of us. He has no legal rights and has never offered one cent of support whatsoever, nor did I demand any. I wanted to make this clear from the outset, to protect Mitch more than anything."

Doctor Harrison held his hand up to stop the legal counsel from responding. "Let me say, your nobility is to be commended. Had I have known what was going on with my nursing students earlier, I would have been more of a mother hen to them instead of letting the fox guard the henhouse, so to speak."

Joyce shifted forward in her seat. "Charles Harrison, it is beneath a man of your vision to sit here and play the if-only-I-had-known game. You are the quintessential success story of our high school graduating class and cannot take the blame for every rascally deed that darkens the clinic's doorway. This community needed this clinic and you brought it to us with great results. And now you are poised to become a different kind of hero, one wrought through the rigors of the legal system."

"I'm convinced that Ms. Lancaster has struck upon a greater truth here," Judge Stallings added. "Blame must be tethered to the guilty party in this matter, and no one else. It is my full intent to focus on that goal from this moment forward. The law will protect the innocent as minds more noble than mine originally intended."

Cami filtered the words through her mind as they

trickled down to her heart. The strength of the law remained on her side, drawing a line in the sand between guilt and innocence, perpetrator and victim. She traced her fingertips along the table's edge as though setting the line onto a real plane of existence. She would be safe on her side of the line. God would ensure it.

The judge glanced down at his portfolio. "A paternity test will be necessary at this point."

Mr. Harrison cleared his throat, his gaze questioning Cami through bushy eyebrows.

Cami knew there was only one answer. "It would be our privilege. I explained to Mitch that a magic wand is going to allow him to slay the bad guy today, so he's ready to participate. Doctor Harrison has volunteered to conduct the swab tests and fix the DNA samples."

Joyce got up and left the room to retrieve Mitch, and Cami fortified herself with a deep breath in the interim.

"Let me remark that you won't be sorry for moving forward," Judge Stallings replied. "I'll help you protect Mitch, as he is truly pivotal in getting these charges to stick."

Cami nodded as the boy appeared through the doorway, all innocent-eyed and apprehensive.

Doctor Harrison pushed his chair back. "How about we go earn a lollipop?"

Cami stood to join them. *What a nice way to sugarcoat the ugly truth.* To her surprise, she felt wholly in the moment, her legs sturdy as she began her journey of redemption.

~

Holt questioned the situation, looking right and left. "There's no way out for me, is there?"

Donnie's eyes crinkled which cracked his poker face expression. In a deft move, his freckled hand took the double-stacked black chips and gained access to the back row where a red chip went sailing off the board in a blaze of defeat.

Big Tom hunkered over the game board, barely able to control his tendency to interfere. "I better teach you how to hold your own a little better than that."

Donnie cleared the remaining game pieces. "Like you can do any better half the time."

Holt folded his hands together as a crow landed beside the picnic table searching for crumbs. "I came out to discuss something with you gentlemen today."

Tom shook the waxed paper that had held his sandwich and the bird came closer to inspect the offer.

"I'm trying to help a friend establish a work co-op at his warehouse to provide some daytime work credit for those of us unemployed at the moment. This whole plan is just getting underway. But before I try to line it up, I wanted to gauge your interest in participating in something productive."

Big Tom wiped his mouth on his sleeve. "Sounds interesting to me."

The creek gurgled beyond the picnic table. Holt let it provide its pleasant distraction while the men contemplated the possibilities.

Donnie's eyes squinted with closer inspection. "What sort of production is it?"

"Stone Traders is the name of the business," Holt replied. "They take rocks from around the world—beautiful rocks—then saw them down, sort them into collections, and ship them out to distributors for selling to the public. I toured there earlier today and found it amazing what comes through their doors. But the main guy works by himself and has a backlog of crates filled with huge rocks. He definitely needs help, so I'm trying to set up a way to get him some."

"I've never been afraid of heavy work." Big Tom ran his hand over his beard stubble. "But if this warehouse isn't someplace I can walk to, I'm not sure I can go for it."

"I'll have to work on transportation as I get this lined up," Holt replied.

"He gonna pay us?" Donnie asked, ever the skeptic.

"Maybe eventually, but to start with, I'm looking at getting this program a sponsor. We'd set up an account at Save Always in your names and you'd earn store credit by working. Does that sound enticing?" The crow cawed and pecked below the table, distracting him while the men exchanged glances.

"Just like that old crow, a man's got to eat," Big Tom replied. "If I could get credit at a food store for myself, why that would be more than enough incentive for me to join up. I don't sit out here playing checkers all day because I want to."

"You could labor during the week and relax on the weekends, just like every other working man," Holt said. "The program might start out slow at first, like every other day until we can gauge how much work there is to be done. You guys could help me tweak things until it becomes a hand-in-glove fit. You know, someone needs the help, and the helpers need work. It has to balance out to be a win-win for both you and the owner."

Donnie began to reset the game board with meticulous care. "Maybe I could make up those collections. I could turn it into a continuous game of checkers to keep the work enjoyable."

"There you go, already thinking a move ahead of me." Holt offered Donnie his hand across the table. Big Tom arched back in a belly laugh and reached for his other hand, which made Holt the center point connecting the two men. He became a bridge of sorts, somewhat tenuous, but he'd spanned a gap of worthlessness toward something more productive.

~

Cami put Mitch back in his waiting spot with permission to enjoy his candy treat while the others reconvened in the conference room. She kissed his head and backtracked, closing the door behind her. A blank sheet of paper rested in front of her seat as she got situated. She couldn't deny the relief she felt to be taking action at long last.

Judge Stallings glanced over his portfolio for details. "We need to anticipate building our case against the defendant. One thing we need to consider is the possibility that there might be more victims out there."

"We had an attractive front desk receptionist resign last month for no apparent reason," Doctor Harrison said.

"I have to agree, that struck me as really odd," Cami replied. "On Friday she wished me a great weekend and, on Monday, she didn't come back in. Bo flirted with her all the time, too, like he's doing with her replacement."

The director made a throaty noise announcing his

displeasure as the legal counsel nodded toward the sheet of paper in front of her. "Write down the names of anyone who could have been a target," the judge said. "We'll have to use a measure of confidentiality at this point, as it's early in our investigation."

Cami recorded the receptionist's name, but was soon distracted.

The clinic director stood and began pacing the room, his face tight with concern.

Judge Stallings tapped the edge of his papers on the tabletop. "Even with so much as one more case against him, I think the board might find themselves in a position to request administrative leave for Doctor Ballard, given the professional setting of the abuse."

"Our quarterly board meeting is this Thursday evening," Doctor Harrison replied. "Believe me, I'm mentally amending my agenda, even as we speak."

Joyce began to rummage in her purse. "Would it necessarily have to be abuse of a sexual nature?" She punched the phone's screen as the director walked up behind her. She proceeded to disclose a series of incriminating photos with the slide of her fingertip.

Cami recognized her own dining area and felt the blood drain from her face. Holt soon appeared as the object of the recorded trespass. Graphic, the last photo captured him taking Bo's fist to his mouth. She had to look away to maintain her composure.

"This dates back to two days ago." Joyce's voice quivered through the rendering. An emotional explosion occurred behind their seats, as the clinic's director detonated at the hideous reality unfolding under his watch.

Cami covered her ears to block the string of

invectives as his disbelief gave way to sheer anger. She had nothing but empathy for the executive, as she had already brooded over the unfairness of it all for a rather lengthy period. In seconds, the legal counsel crossed to view the phone scenes. The room seemed lopsided with concern. Joyce repeated the sequence of snapshots for his benefit.

The seasoned lawyer became the next person to blanch. "I'll need those submitted as evidence." He straightened and regarded the director without speaking a word.

Cami recognized that justice only had only one voice, that of the victim. "I'll have Mr. Ellis fill out his full testimony." She penned Holt's name onto her list of possible abuse victims. "At this rate, we might need a few more blank sheets."

~

Holt exited the police station, exhausted from his pursuit of transportation but elated at the prospect of gaining help. Officer Gaines had introduced him to his captain, who explained that a coalition of cooperative agencies might be the hub that could put wheels on the jobs program. He only hoped that Chris was having similar success with his boss, which would open the warehouse door to workers. His heels clicked along the sidewalk until a car slowed behind him and drew his attention.

A boy waved him down from the back seat. "Want a ride, mister?"

When Cami pulled the car to the curb, Holt's heart skipped a beat at her radiant expression. "Yeah. I'd like that a lot." He slapped the boy's hand as he walked around front to get in. "I wonder who's had the most success?' He baited Cami as he buckled the seatbelt.

"You can hardly top what we've been through." Cami flashed a beaming smile. "But you might be surprised to learn that you've helped win the battle on both fronts."

Joyce flashed her phone at him with discretion, the sucker punch captured in photographic accuracy.

He pulled in an airy breath, his shock genuine.

"Now how do you feel about recording your testimony right alongside mine?" Cami mashed the accelerator as though to get him moving forward on it right away.

Holt leaned back and touched the diminished scab on his lip cut. *No pain, no gain.* His eyes flitted closed under the soothing breeze of the air conditioner, and somewhere on the road back to the duplex he passed the point of no return.

Chapter 14

Cami glanced up from the glider on the back patio as Aunt Joyce slid her door open to let Holt escape with two glasses of iced tea. Mitch gave her a quick wave and darted back into the kitchen's interior where preparations were underway for their last dinner together. She accepted the glass and stopped the swaying motion long enough to allow him to sit down beside her, then pushed off again to float through the evening. She took a sip and let the coolness trickle down her throat.

Holt stretched his legs out to relax. "Today was unforgettable in so many ways."

She laid her head back on his arm. "What will you remember the most?" Dusk faded the day against the dark crag of mountain in the forefront, a jigsaw puzzle scene.

Ice cubes jingled against his glass as he took a sip

and gave her question some thought. "Well, it started with the way you looked at me this morning, as I haven't exactly garnered many catcalls recently."

"Guilty as charged." She giggled without being able to corral it and turned to look at him. "I think you're handsome, scratches and all. There, I've said it out loud. Holt Ellis is a fox."

"Now I'm embarrassed for being truthful." He mouthed his glass to catch an ice cube. "You go next," he mumbled.

"I fell into a deeper admiration of God's creation at the rock shop." She pulled her feet up beneath her and scooted under his arm. "And I have a new favorite rock that someone dear to my heart gave me because he knew I would like it. Funny how something as inanimate as a rock can breathe new life into your spirit." She hoped to see deeper into his soul. "What else struck you?"

He leaned over and kissed the curve of her shoulder, then relaxed against the padded glider. "That Chris guy struck me as the real deal. I hope my jobless buddies can link up with him for something life-changing for all involved. It's wild how God just impresses that kind of thing on my heart and then my brain kicks in, trying to figure out a way to make it happen."

"Something has occurred to me several times, so I'm going to put it out there and let you consider it. I truly think your marketing expertise has been coaxed in the wrong direction. What I think you'd really excel at is a career with humanity at the core, not a product. What if you marketed people, not products, Holt? You're a natural connector. Aunt Joyce pointed that out to me, saying it's like a spiritual gift. So maybe you should be working for a nonprofit somewhere, instead of pitching dog food and the like." A long sigh followed her revelation amid more tinkling from the glass. She sipped her tea, confident she was on target.

"I honestly thought of majoring in social work, but gravitated toward marketing because it had more of a business application. At the time, I'd hoped to be a sharp young professional making a mark on this world. Who knew the corporate world would see marketing as the most dispensable department when it came time to lay off staff and get lean?"

"Your flair for it becomes obvious right away, so maybe there's a way to combine the two strengths into something truly magnificent."

"Thanks for helping me dream, Cami, as it feels like I'm getting my feet back under me for the first time in a great long while. Here's something else that I'll keep as a memory maker from today—that entire bit with Mitch at the piano."

She jerked around and looked at him, her mouth wide open, tea sloshing from her glass. "Was that a moment out of time, or what? You bet I was busting with pride and wanted to say something like 'that's my boy, underprivileged and still making the most out of life!' An angel must have hushed me down, but on the inside, let me tell you, I may have busted a seam."

Holt laughed, caught her chin in his hand, and gave her a look charged with affection. "Mitch is not underprivileged in the least, because he gets to spend every day with you. And that should be enough incentive to grow a fatherless boy into a contributing member of society in whatever field he chooses. But for this day, he gave those ladies at the museum something to cherish—and it pierced my heart through and through.”

A warm tear ran down her cheek as she shared admiration of her son with someone else who could be trusted with it. The sensation transported her to a place that she’d never been before. “You really know how to get to a girl, Holt.” She hoped her honesty would somehow mesmerize him. Maybe the purple haze of dusk worked to her favor, because he drew her into his arms for a full embrace. It made for another remembrance on an unforgettable day—a life fully lived, even after the sun found the backside of the mountain.

“You’re incredible,” Holt whispered, right before he kissed her former regrets away.

She stayed there tucked in his admiration, gliding through the evening until a knock announced that dinner was ready. “Let’s go launch a bon voyage party.” She ran her fingers through his tousled hair.

He grabbed her glass and motioned for her to go first. When she paused at the sliding door, he whispered in her ear and brought up goose bumps. “Meet me back at the glider to say goodnight, and don’t forget to bring your candle.”

She went velvet on the inside and found a new appreciation for his sensitivity. “Only if you behave.” The chastisement was for her own benefit. Now if she could follow through.

~

“That roast was huge, Joyce.” Holt wiped the last trace of gravy from his mouth as Mitch lined up peas on the tines of his fork and rolled them into his bottomless vault.

Cami cleaned up the last remains of her creamed potatoes. "And cooked to perfection."

Joyce shifted the carving knife onto the platter for transfer off the table. "Well, I wanted to leave Holt some leftovers so he wouldn't have to depend on his bachelor skills too soon. Mitchell, don't forget your roll." The boy looked up and fisted the crescent roll into his mouth. The hostess stifled a laugh but her eyes held only love.

"Tell us about your plans to travel across America." Holt sketched a sky-trail with his fork. "Which route have you picked?"

Cami smiled across from him and toyed with a sautéed apple slice that had been orphaned on her plate. Mitch reached over and stole it from her fork, then gobbled it down.

"I've selected the northern route, mainly to meet a distant cousin in Michigan's Door County to see the cherry trees in bloom," Joyce replied. "She claims their spring is running late this year, which I'll use to my full advantage. Then I'll slide through the Pennsylvania Dutch country, maybe catch a quilt show or two, and then bounce back north on my way to Maine."

Cami leaned toward her aunt. "Who's this mystery friend that wants you to come early? Holt seems to know more about this than me, which will never do."

"Oh, let's not make more of it than there is. An old friend named Mason lives down the coast from the cottage and wants me to get there in time for a music festival at nearby Bowdoin College. It's strictly a shared passion for classical music, I assure you."

"Aha, the plot thickens." Holt arched his brow with

innuendo. "Maybe just music, but maybe something more…"

Joyce pushed away from the table. "You lovebirds are precious, aren't you? All submerged in love and trying to drag everyone else underwater with you."

"I don't get it." Mitch steadied another load of peas on his fork. "Birds don't even swim. Maybe you should say 'love-fish' instead."

"Well, is this Mason married, or not?" Cami blinked, her interest sincere.

Holt gazed between the two women and suddenly wished he could shrink to the size of one of the peas Mitch had dropped.

Joyce propped her hands on her hips and gave a coy glance their way. "Mason is a widower, for your information. He claims that he's totally happy in that predicament, and I wouldn't expect anything to have changed over the winter. But if you'd like to speculate in that direction, I'm willing to let you daydream all you want."

"I think it's safe to say that you can't rule anything out, given how God makes things click at the right time in the right place." Holt stood, picked up his smeared-clean plate, and handed it to her at the sink.

Cami looked up at her with softness tempering her gaze. "Keep your heart open, Aunt Joyce. Promise me that, if you will."

Joyce ran the rinse water in the sink and then paused. "Okay, my heart is open but my ears are going to the concert expressly for their own enjoyment."

"As I found out today at the spontaneous piano recital, the human body seems to be all connected," Holt replied. "What often goes in the ears frequently comes out of the heart."

"Touché, my dear summer tenant. I'll have cherry blossom eyes and violin ears, and even allow Mason to hold my hand if he wants to." Joyce's capitulation seemed halfhearted. "Silly business, this love."

"And don't forget my visit to the land of chocolate where the streetlights are shaped like kisses," Mitch said, his peas now demolished.

"Yes, I plan to keep that promise to take you to Hershey, Pennsylvania some day," Joyce replied. "I'm just waiting for you to be old enough to remember it."

The boy squished up his facial features. "I remember everything."

"Then how did that spelling test come home with a grade of 'B' on it yesterday?" Cami asked.

Mitch's face flinched like a kid with his hand in the candy jar. "Well, I meant everything that's important. You really can't be digging around in a man's hidden stuff, Mom. I crunched that paper into the bottom of my backpack." He stood in protest and took his plate to the sink.

"Oh, yes I can dig." Cami rose and handed Joyce her plate. Swapping the gesture, Joyce passed a plate back to her.

Holt rolled his eyes. "Blueberry cheesecake? This is quite a send-off, you to Maine and me to fat-and-happy land."

"Glad I could oblige." Joyce brought a knife and a small stack of dessert plates with her to the table. The graham-crusted treat took center stage between them as they exchanged looks of admiration. Mitch rinsed his plate and ran back to the table to be dessert eligible.

"You truly are going to be missed around here,"

Holt said.

Joyce's top lip quivered just the slightest bit. "And what could be better than that?"

Cami bent and gave her a huge hug, which Mitch instantly had to get in on.

Holt reached over and found her hand amid the melee, and they all held onto what they had to let go.

~

Cami pulled the door closed as she balanced the candle. "Sorry I couldn't get out here sooner. I let Mitch stay up an hour later on weekend nights, as long as he's been good."

"Joyce and I had some last-minute things to deal with, like a leaky faucet," Holt replied.

"Always a conservationist." She settled on the glider beside him. The candle found its place on a plant stand. Cami adjusted it closer to better enjoy the flickering light.

"And a notoriously light sleeper, which makes a dripping faucet my public enemy number one. I shouldn't have any problem tonight though, as it's been a full day."

"Don't nod out on me yet, as I have some things I haven't addressed with you. Nothing as threatening as a dripping faucet, mind you, but there are some other shadowy figures out there, just the same." When he dropped vertical to put his head in her lap, she sank her fingers into his new haircut as the night sang around them.

Holt shifted. "Tell me about your lurking shadows. Tell me everything."

"I spotted Bo's Beemer in the playground parking lot this afternoon when we came back to check the mailbox," Cami replied.

"How unusual is that. Does he try to visit Mitch?"

"No, it's extremely unusual, I mean to the point of being spooky, Holt. Bo never drops by. My worry is that he may be stalking Mitchell for some insane reason."

"Whoa now. Don't let your imagination get carried away. Let's be rational and think this through." He reached up for her.

She laced her fingers into his, grateful for his stability. "Okay, the first time, when he met Mitch on the playground, was right after his fight with you, like he was busting you for entering his territory or something. That's when he labeled you a 'quitter,' which Mitch repeated in his rebellion."

"So maybe the playground offers neutral territory, perfect for collusion."

"Right, beyond my control. I'm trying not to let it grate on my nerves, but the fact that his behavior coincides with the legal action gives me cause to be, well, uncomfortable."

"How soon will Bo be tipped off that something is up at work?"

"The clinic's board of directors meets Thursday night. They could vote to suspend him without pay while the allegations are brought to bear, so we have less than a week to tighten down some boundaries."

"Wow, thanks for letting me know. Joyce wants me to keep a watch over things, and I'd better go into it with both eyes wide open. I want you to feel free to tell me anything that seems remotely suspicious. We'll tackle it together, agreed?" He squeezed her fingers as though to emphasize his offer.

An ominous lump formed in her throat. Cami had something else to say, something she needed to say, and this was the perfect time to say it.

"Holt, I have to speak my heart and tell you what it means to have you in my life." Her voice turned husky-sweet. She bent closer and traced his face with her gaze, the candle flickering close-by. "You've been such a balm to my heart—to help it finally thaw out from its numbness and start feeling again. While it looks like I've been taking care of your scraped up outer wounds, you've really been the healer for my scratch-and-dent inner ones. Between the two of us, though, I want things to be completely genuine. I'm in love with you, Holt, and can hardly wait to see where God takes this incredible friendship he's given us. No matter how crazy things might get, know that I love you."

He sat up without a word and pulled her closer. The space between them evaporated and he sealed the declaration with an unhurried kiss. The night held them together in breathless connection as the glider swayed without friction.

The screen door screeched open and Cami forced herself to look up.

"Mommy? Help me. I have a terrible tummy ache." Mitch stepped through the door and let out a low moan. Holt bolted to his feet at the sound.

Freed for more nurse duty, Cami quelled her resentment at the interruption as she raced to her son's side. At least she'd spoken her heart. The solitary moon would have to hold it in place.

Chapter 15

Cami pulled the foil cap off a strawberry yogurt tub and sat it in front of Mitch. They had finally gotten past the tummy turmoil around midnight, which left her beauty sleep truncated. Nervous about worshipping beside Holt for the first time at her church, she had already changed outfits twice. A glance down revealed a strawberry-pink spatter on her latest choice, a green knit dress. She rushed to the sink to sponge away the blob.

"Sounds like Aunt Joyce is getting packed up," Mitch said, his voice weak.

She snapped a paper towel off the roll and blotted the spot on her way to the front door. Holt disappeared under the hood of Aunt Joyce's car, doing some last minute maintenance. Without hesitation, Cami trailed out the door and crossed the front lawn to greet him. "Good morning, Mr. Mechanic." She bent under the hood as he slid the oil level dipstick out of its shaft.

"Paper towel," he replied. After he cleared the residue, he shoved the dipstick back down the sleeve and paused to give her a closer look. "You're dressed too nice to be my assistant." He drew the dipstick back out like a sword, glanced at the mark, and returned his saber to its original position. Next he tapped the battery cables and knocked some corrosion crud from the poles. "Looks pretty good in here." At that, he folded in the prop and lowered the hood with a bang.

She took possession of the oily wad between two newly painted fingernails. "I hope you rested well last night." She blushed as he gave her a head-to-toe once-over, like she had become part of the diagnostics package. When he smiled, she held her breath for his reply.

"Umm. Looks pretty good out here, too." He held two greasy palms up as if to defend himself. "Only, you seem to be leaking transmission fluid out of your fingertips."

She gave him a testy look. "Grease monkeys with a warped sense of humor don't get fingers run through their hair under the moonlight."

"Okay, I take that last comment back. But I must say that pink fuzzy slippers don't really go with green and blue flowers for church clothes, at least not where I come from."

Cami gasped. She'd not given one thought to her footwear when she popped out of the house. She turned and retreated in a full blush, her hemline swishing with her speedy gait as his laughter filled the front yard. Maybe he could stand an improvement or two as well. "Lose the cow shirt for church," she replied, right before punching the front door handle.

Holt came a few steps closer and picked at the cow motif. "Hey, what's wrong with this? Chick-fil-A is a Christian-owned company, not to mention the epicenter of sheer marketing genius."

The front door banged closed as her only response. She made a beeline to her closet and spent the next few minutes trying on every pair of shoes inside. She finally decided on the peep-toed wedges, the ones that best accentuated her transmission fluid-colored toenails. Just let him say something about that.

Mitch appeared at her bedroom door. "All done, Mom."

"Fine, honey. Go brush your teeth. Let's hope that yogurt stays down while we're in church. I'll get your Bible when I snag the car keys." She soon thought of one more nurse-type check she'd better run, so she followed him to his bathroom. Glancing at him in the mirror as he loaded his toothbrush, she slid a loving hand across his forehead lifting his bangs out of the way. His temperature felt normal. The tummy ache wasn't from a bug. "I'll be praying for you today, for God to restore your good health so you can go to school tomorrow. Who knows, they may announce the slogan contest winner, and you'll be there to hear your name called."

"That would be sweet," he replied through a sudsy froth building inside his mouth.

Cami kissed his hair and disappeared to go brush her teeth. Maybe she'd get a touch of lip gloss on, a demure tone that wouldn't raise any cynical comments.

~

Holt stared ahead at the contemporary edifice of

the building. "I'm honored to be worshipping with your family today."

"You'll like it here," Joyce replied, as she buttoned her short-sleeved jacket. "The people are nice in a genuine sort of way, not stuffy. I'll introduce you around if there's time between services."

"We're here for the Sunday school hour," Cami said. She bent to straighten Mitch's shirttail. "You'll have to hang with me, as the chairs in Mitch's class are a bit small for you."

"And my class is restricted to ladies, darling," Joyce added. "The young professionals' class is the best fit for you anyway. Mitchell, try to learn something new about God this morning. Remember that I'll be asking you about your lesson on the way home today."

"Yes, ma'am," the boy replied. "I'll pay attention."

Holt felt the immediate tug to rescue the boy from the spotlight, so he patted him on the back as he stepped up the curb. "Me too, Mitch. I'll do my best to pay attention, too. You can ask me questions afterwards, like giving me a pop quiz."

"Golly, I hate pop quizzes." His chubby cheeks sagged.

Cami crooked a corrective brow at Holt as he opened the door. "Could that be a cow's ear I'm seeing above your top button?"

He self-consciously straightened his collar tabs. "Um, maybe. Is this a multiple choice pop quiz?"

She flashed him a glossy smile as she turned down a lengthy hallway while Joyce took Mitch the opposite direction.

"Bye, Holt." Mitch gave a parting wave.

Holt saluted his departure and stepped up to walk

beside Cami. A family filed past delivering their children, and a sense of belonging poured over him. He looked up and saw a rough crucifix hanging on the end wall, surrounded with blocks of stained glass. Somehow, the striking combination affected him further, and he prepared his heart to worship through learning. Unaware that he had stopped, Cami's arm slipped through his elbow as she prompted him one room further.

"This feels right," he whispered, the cross ever before him.

She glanced at the cross and pulled him toward the doorway. "Yes, it does."

The way she looked at him made Holt lighter than air. They were sharing their faith together, and what greater test of compatibility could there be? It was a question with only one correct answer, but he didn't suppose it would be on the pop test that followed.

~

Classmates shared prayer requests from their hearts, without making petty demands for Jesus' attention. This was always Cami's favorite part of class. The leader had just opened the floor for requests, and her girlfriend Grace had gotten the ball rolling with a petition for safe travels.

"My aunt Joyce leaves today for Maine," Cami added. "So please remember her for the next few days as she drives through the heart of America. And could we lift up Mitch? He had a stomach ache last night." The leader recorded her two requests, which created a slight pause.

"I'd like to ask God for a full-time job," Holt said. "I'm a marketing professional and it's been tough for awhile to find something in Golden. This is where my heart is, so I'd rather stay local, if possible. And pray for my work with the area's homeless, as I'm launching a work-for-food program at a local business this week." He dropped his head as he braced forward, elbows on his thighs.

Grace leaned forward in her seat. "Am I recognizing you from the newspaper? Are you that missing Bicycle Man?"

"Yes, I'm Holt Ellis, Bicycle Man. Now you can see why I've been missing. I had a little accident coming down Lookout Mountain, which is how Cami and I not-so-gently met." He lifted his scraped left arm and garnered a few sympathetic laughs.

"No wonder you want to stay local," Grace added. "But God already knew that, so I bet he's working on something one-of-a-kind, just for you. That's how I'm going to pray." Others murmured their agreement.

"Thanks so much, all of you," Holt replied. "It's been a hard six months, but I'm feeling God draw me nearer to him, like a reminder of what's really important in life."

"I should have let you teach class this morning," the leader said with humor in his voice as he recorded the last request. "Any more before we go to God in prayer?"

Cami glanced over at Holt. His prayer time had already started as his eyes were shut. She empathized with his state of dependency, even with only a half night of sleep behind her eyelids. Within minutes, class adjourned and the guys stood to shake hands.

Grace led her aside as she pulled her purse strap onto the crown of her shoulder. "If I go bike riding up the mountain today, can I come home with one of those?"

Cami stifled her laugh and picked a piece of fluff off her friend's blouse. "Totally a God thing," she replied as she stole a furtive glance at Holt. "But just in case, try to make a softer entrance than I managed, so the pain and suffering part can be eliminated."

"Well, since I'm not a nurse and God knows I'm super squeamish about blood, I'll anticipate another means of merging two paths into one. Maybe my business trip to Colorado Springs is just the thing, since it's a real Christian hotspot."

"Hold that thought, girlfriend," Cami replied. "I'll be praying for you." A hand touched the small of her back and she instinctively stepped toward the door, curling a finger wave at her confidante.

"Great support group." Holt stuffed his hands in his pockets at the admission.

She bumped her shoulder against his as they walked up the hall to the auditorium. "You fit right in, Holt. That felt good to me."

"Me, too. Now what did your girlfriend have to say that I couldn't hear?"

"Oh, she wants a Bicycle Man, too—only without the bloody meeting-up scene."

"That's another kind of prayer request," he replied, "one that goes unspoken."

"But the Holy Spirit hears the heart, for which I am most grateful."

He slipped his hand into hers. "And now you're about to hear my singing, for which you might not be as grateful."

It struck her how marvelous the discovery process

was. "Well, since you've seen me in my slippers, I think we're ready for that phase of closeness."

"Hey, introduce me to your pastor before we sit down."

"I'd be honored to, if only you could make that cow's ear disappear." She gave him a slow wink and turned the corner where a spacious gathering room opened like the belly of a whale. Holt made a low whistle of appreciation and she enjoyed watching him scan the cavernous wood-beamed ceiling. "We call it the auditorium instead of a sanctuary, because we believe each person's heart is the true sanctuary where the Lord abides."

He tucked at his T-shirt and straightened his collar. "I like that word choice almost as much as I like this building. Maybe my singing will get lost up there and mingle with the rest."

"Wait until you hear Mitch. Let's just say that boy will never need a microphone."

"Then I'm sitting beside him."

"Oh no, you're not. Remember, he's been sick. That's the last thing you need right now. You're beside me on the outside, just like the protector you are."

"Okay, I'll try to hold the offering tray off of you, Princess Cami-lot."

"Do we have royalty in our midst?" an eavesdropping man asked with joviality. Cami looked up and proceeded to turn ten shades of red. He offered Holt his hand.

"Good morning, Pastor Reed. This is my friend, Holt Ellis."

"Nice to meet you, Holt." He gave his hand a second shake. "I've been waiting for some man with a lick of sense to see what a treasure Cami is. Since you're calling her a princess, I'll consider that an answered prayer."

Cami pulled Holt toward the auditorium. "More than one answered prayer."

"Come again soon," the pastor replied as they mixed between other attendees up the aisle.

She paused beside the row where her family typically sat. "Well, he certainly won't forget you any time soon."

Holt squared around to face her fully and motioned his hand up and down his scraped exterior. "Like this is a body anyone could forget," he replied with a laugh. "Honestly though, I can't wait to hear the sermon."

A flutter of Sunday school papers announced Mitch's arrival as Aunt Joyce motioned them into the row. "Me, too, so could you stop taking up so much space and let me sit down? I claim the aisle."

"I'll go first and fight off any errant ushers." Holt shuffled his feet down the row. "How are you feeling, Mitch?"

The boy birthed a huge yawn. "A little sleepy, now that you mention it."

Cami trailed Holt while restraining her son to wait his turn. "Good. Why should this Sunday be any different?" She nodded to several women in the row ahead as she settled into her seat and let the cushioned pew do its best Sunday welcome. Mitch squirmed in against her, surrendering his papers to her Bible. Aunt Joyce settled at the end of the row and passed down her bulletin for their use. Cami exhaled and soon allowed the announcements on the overhead screen to keep her thoughts occupied. Here they sat in church together, nothing short of a miracle.

~

Holt heaved the last oversized suitcase into the trunk and slammed it with a grunt. Locked arm-in-arm, the women strolled down the driveway. When Cami rested her head on her aunt's shoulder, the intimacy of the scene touched his heart as he waited by the car. Mitch came out of the front door with a bang and waved a sign he had colored for the occasion. Joyce bent to receive it. She clutched it to her chest and enfolded the boy in a three-way hug.

He opened the car door as the driver approached, teary-eyed but otherwise ready for departure. She placed the artwork on the dashboard as Cami gave her one last protracted hug. He studied the masterpiece, where a mother-and-son combination waved goodbye inside a giant heart. In the corner, a man on a bike also waved. At least he was in the picture now, if not yet fully inside the dubious boy's heart.

Chapter 16

Cami stared at the packed waiting room and wondered why Mondays arrived with so many challenges. She called the name on the file and a mother with two young children responded. She smiled in sympathy with the weariness in the woman's eyes. Had it not been for yesterday's late afternoon rain shower that put her to sleep in Holt's arms, she'd likely look much the same.

Cami halted at the scales. "Rough weekend, I'm guessing." The mother nodded and guided the preschooler onto the platform. She jotted down the weight reading and lowered the height rod as the ruddy-cheeked boy moved under it. Again she made note of the reading and led the family to the first exam room. Once the mother sat down, the baby in her arms started a fuss. "Can you tell me what he's been experiencing?"

The woman pulled out a set of plastic keys and

jangled them in front of the baby. "The fever started Saturday night and I couldn't seem to get it down," she replied. "Then Sunday afternoon, he started throwing up. From that point on, we were all miserable."

She wrote the symptoms onto the form. "I've been down that same lane recently. What about an earache, sore throat, or nasal congestion?"

"Bad sore throat," she replied. "He had a hard time swallowing this morning."

"Okay then, the doctor will likely want to swab his throat for strep. Let me get his temperature first and then I'll go get him in here."

"Thank you so much," the mother replied, her face softening.

"You're very welcome," Cami assured her. "Just keep the baby away from big brother until we get this figured out so I won't have to see you again later in the week." The mom shifted the baby to her far hip as the chair scooted toward the door. The temperature reading came in above normal. Cami recorded it, and with a sincere smile she popped out the door.

A commotion down the hall caught her off guard. It escalated quickly to a shouting match, and Cami ran toward the source, hoping to calm things down. She heard another outburst and recognized Doctor Harrison's voice reverberating from what sounded like the staff lounge. As she approached, she bumped into the new receptionist who looked like she was running from a ghost. When the young woman pivoted around her, Cami noticed her lipstick had smeared onto her cheek.

"Fix your lipstick before you go out there," Cami called behind her as she pressed ahead. She rounded the doorway and discovered Bo, crouched and facing off against Doctor Harrison across the break room table in a scene right out of a high school wrestling match. Shocked, her mouth fell open as she read the enraged expression contorting the director's face.

"Doctor Ballard, your behavior infuriates me beyond the point of self-control," the aging man yelled. "Have you no decency at all?"

Cami walked in with her hands in the air like a referee. "Doctors, please. Our patients can hear you…" The director gave her a blank stare, and then backed off, trembling against the water dispenser. Bo turned to her with disdain. Evidence that filled in the details of what she had speculated screamed from the shoulder of his lab coat. A mulberry stain matched the receptionist's lipstick color. A familiar feeling of personal betrayal started up her throat but she took a breath and forced it back down.

"You're supposed to be here conducting your profession, one held by the community in the highest regard," Doctor Harrison said. Each word dripped with venom. "Since it appears that you are incapable of maintaining your professional demeanor over your… your… insatiable philandering, I hereby place you on administrative leave without pay until the board meets Thursday night to address the matter of your continued role."

Cami clenched her teeth together so her jaw wouldn't drop open and give Bo the satisfaction of having outright shocked her. This judicious ending proved inevitable, but the crash that hastened it certainly was not. She knew Bo, and he would lash back. The hairs on the back of her neck stood straight up at the fear-filled realization that she was well within the splash zone of his toxic sphere of influence. Holt's support popped into her mind and she discovered the courage to stand her ground. Her resolve must have shown in her eyes, because an air of perplexity flashed across Bo's face.

Doctor Harrison folded his arms across his heaving chest. "You may leave the premises now, Dr. Ballard."

Cami stood with arms akimbo to echo the director's ultimatum. Bo clasped the open lapels of his lab coat and strode out of the room. His sinister gaze locked on her as he exited.

She couldn't exhale until the back door clicked closed behind him.

Doctor Harrison approached her with nerves so jangled his hands were shaking. "Well, the excrement has certainly hit the proverbial fan." He shook his head. "Maybe it's better this way, come to think of it. This will force the board to take action one way or the other, which they are often too complacent to do." He formed a fist with his right hand and smacked it into his left palm. "This might even be enough to strip him of his license."

In spite of her loyalty for the director's position, the fallout of Bo being gone hit her between the shoulder blades and stole her next breath. "Now we're a doctor short, with a waiting room full of patients." The clinical detachment she had mustered wouldn't last under this level of pressure. "It's barely ten o'clock and we haven't seen half of them yet."

Dr. Harrison pulled himself back to full height. "Tell me where to start."

"Room One is a preschool boy with a possible

strep throat."

"All right, then. I'll take the swab and you go ahead with the next patient."

Cami walked him to the doorway. "Yes, sir. And may I say you did the absolute right thing. Bo brought this catastrophe on himself. What we do next will have everything to do with justice. Don't let it be personal or you become the victim and he wins again."

The director looked at her and his eyes held a gleam. "You're starting to remind me of your wonderful aunt." He patted her hand.

"I accept that as a high compliment, sir. You know I'm with you on this until the end."

"And today, I'll trust you to keep me moving through my paces." He disappeared down the hall.

Cami had a sudden impulse to call Holt and tell him about Bo, but a crying baby geared up and she tucked the thought away and became a nurse once again.

~

Holt sat in the glider, which seemed more than half empty without Cami. The morning sun had evaporated the late rain from the patio's surface, leaving everything clean and refreshed. He had read several chapters from the guest room Bible and spent some time in prayer, even remembering to include the Sunday school class requests. His gaze dropped to the legal pad where he'd jotted some notes and flow diagrams detailing the work-for-food program for his homeless friends. Maybe he'd call Chris later to fill him in on his progress. Holt glanced at Cami's half of the duplex where the only viable phone lived. If only he could get a job, he'd have a cell phone again—plus a whole lot more.

To his immediate delight, the family cat came to the back glass and began kneading with its claws. The feline paced in front of the doorframe and meowed so loud he could hear it from the glider. It occurred to him that Cami might have forgotten to feed the poor guy, since Mitch had been recovering from his upset stomach. He stood, slid the door open, and caught the cooperative pet. "All right, Scrubs. You're not homeless, but I'll feed you anyway." He forced the screen closed with his foot.

He scanned the countertop and found an empty cat bowl in the sink. He placed the cat on the counter and proceeded to rinse out the bowl, then searched for the cat's food in the cabinets below. He found a sack beyond the dishwasher and shook it to get the cat's attention. Scrubs licked the milk from Mitch's half-finished cereal bowl. Holt questioned whether the counter might be forbidden territory for the furry pet, so he poured a generous torrent of dry nuggets into the bowl and set it on the floor.

"Come on, boy. Let's get you set up over by your usual spot." Holt swept up the trespassing feline with one hand, grabbed the bowl, and headed for the laundry room to complete the circuit between hunger and food provision. The cat went to the food right away and provided him the instant reward he'd been hoping for. The acrid scent of a neglected litter box caught his attention next, and he surveyed the situation. In ten minutes, he had completed another good deed and left the laundry room to seek out his next conquest.

The phone rang as he dried his hands, which caught him off guard. He checked the caller ID display at saw that it was Mitch's elementary school. His stomach tightened, knowing the boy had been sick over the weekend. A second ring seemed more insistent than the first and he decided to pick up the receiver.

"Walsh residence," he answered, glancing around the room. His gaze landed on the newspaper article featuring Bicycle Man on the door of the refrigerator, which lent him some confidence that he somehow belonged here.

"Hello. This is Tammy from the main office. Mitchell's teacher wanted you to know that Save Always has asked for a special assembly this afternoon to announce the winner of its slogan contest. It seems their CEO happens to be in town and wants to bestow the honor himself. Mitchell is a top-five finalist in the competition. His teacher wanted to make sure that Cami could be there for the big moment."

Holt couldn't squelch the grin pulling across his scratched cheek. "Yes, ma'am. We'd love to be there. Exactly what time is the assembly? Cami doesn't get off until three o'clock."

"Let's see. That would be during our seventh hour, which starts at three-thirty. I hope that gives you enough time to make it over here. Please go straight to the auditorium. Since we'll have several families coming in, we can waive the sign-in protocol this once."

"Thank you, Tammy. You've just made me a happy man."

"Good luck to Mitchell and have a nice day. Goodbye."

Holt replaced the receiver as the possibilities raced through his head. If Cami came straight home, she'd be late for the assembly. But if she went straight to the school, he'd be left out, unless he was waiting by her car at the end of her shift. That would provide him some exercise and save critical time, too.

He glanced at the clock as Scrubs encircled his ankles. He could call Cami in half an hour and announce the big news. He shuffled over to the sink, grabbed the cereal bowl, and rinsed it out. Mitch must be sky-high to have his slogan selected for the top five.

"Probably a lot like I'm feeling." He whistled as he looked around for his next good deed. The cat meowed and he bent to scratch its back until the creature's body became an arch of total satisfaction. "Oh, yes indeed." His murmur matched the cat's purr. "Now everybody's happy."

~

Cami hunched over the roast beef sandwich. Her feet ached, as it had been nonstop since the blow up earlier, in this very spot. "Lord, please turn this impossible day around. And thank you for this food. Amen." She exhaled and moved her water bottle closer to her plate to leave space for someone else, though she doubted anyone would share her break, given the scarcity of staff. She snatched the plastic wrap off the sandwich's corner and felt an odd quiver on her thigh. Once she realized her cell phone still remained on vibrate from Sunday services, she scrambled to get the device out and answer it.

"Hello there," Holt said. "Hope I'm not bothering you."

"Hey, no bother. I'm on lunch break." She braced the phone on her shoulder so she could nibble at the sandwich.

"I have big news, but let me use this as my opener.

Seems you forgot to feed the cat this morning." He snickered into the receiver. "No worries, though. I've rectified the gross injustice."

"Oh, good grief. Did Scrubs roar loud enough for you to hear him?"

"The offended critter was both heard and seen from where I sat on the glider reading the Bible Joyce lent me."

"Then you've had a quieter morning than mine. Doctor Harrison caught Bo smooching on the receptionist in the break room here around ten this morning and he went ballistic."

"Are you kidding me?"

"Absolutely not. Bo was released from duty and we've got a waiting room full of sick folks backlogged through the afternoon." She took a drink of her water and positioned the sandwich for another attack.

"Well, you have to be off by three o'clock, and that's all there is to it. Hear me out and I think you'll agree. Mitch's school called, so I picked up the receiver, worried that he might be sick again. But it was Tammy from the main office. She invited us to attend the seventh hour assembly when the visiting CEO of Save Always will announce the big winner of the slogan contest. Mitch's entry made the top five, so he's in the running to take the grand prize. Isn't that great?"

"Fantastic," she replied, her mouth chock-full of roast beef. "Now I have to eat faster than ever so I can process all these patients and leave on time."

"Since I'm the boy's senior advertising advisor, he'll need me there, right? I've already come up with a way I can go with you. Don't be surprised to see me waiting by your car when you come out. I'll walk over to the clinic."

"Do me a favor and stay outside, okay?" She chased the request with another mouthful of water. "We have lots of germs swirling inside this place. It might be nice not to have to nurse anyone while I'm off duty." Another portion of sandwich disappeared as she waited for his laugh to roll off the line.

"I think the possession arrow for caregiving is pointing toward me today," he replied. "I'm good at saving you, just ask Scrubs."

"Okay then, bring me a change of clothes when you come, if it isn't too much trouble," she said, to test him. "I don't want my picture taken beside the winner in my bland uniform." A pause ensued and she took a final bite from her lunch and packed the rest away. She heard him clear his throat as he dealt with the personal nature of her request.

"Should I match that ensemble with pink fuzzy slippers, or would you like something more appropriate?"

A smile cracked her face on this otherwise impossible day. Holt was saving her sanity. "Go in my closet and find the white plastic hanger with a pink top and khaki capris on it. Any of my flat sandals will do. The grocery bags are under the sink." She stood and turned to the refrigerator, where she stuffed the remains of her lunch.

"Anything else?" He sounded ready to accept his task.

"Yeah, look both ways before you cross the street," she teased. "I'm going off my shift at three o'clock sharp."

"Let's hope so, anyway. A budding marketing

prodigy will want his mother in attendance when he takes the stage to accept his prize. Should I bring the camera?"

"Oh yes, Holt. It's over by the computer. Okay, I've got to head back to the trenches now." She started to clip the phone closed when she heard him express his love to her. It started a surge that flowed top to bottom, right into her orthopedic nursing shoes. By the end of the hallway, she had fully recharged. She bumped into Doctor Harrison as he exited his office.

"I've called an old friend." He took the next file off the door to Room One. "He'll be here by one o'clock and you'll get your two-doctor rotation back."

"I really need to be out of here by three o'clock today if at all possible," she replied. "Mitch is in the top five for an award at school and I simply have to be there."

"Let's make sure it happens." He disappeared into the exam room with a slight smile.

Cami walked back out toward the front desk and counted the patients as she went. When she approached the desk, the receptionist still appeared quite shaken. Maybe some compassion would help the situation. "Listen. These people are all counting on you to do the very best job possible," she said, her tone low and steady. "I think you can provide that level of service, don't you?"

"Yes, ma'am," the young woman replied in shaky compliance.

Cami nodded to extend her some grace and took the next file. She called the name of her next medical challenge and reduced the waiting list by one more patient.

Chapter 17

Holt found a cadence with his pace as he tackled the last residential street before the route turned commercial. Late spring burst around him from tidy front yards and filled his steps with vigor. To think he almost missed this rhapsody of life by giving up too soon. He would never let himself make that kind of mistake again, God willing. He switched the bag of clothes into his right hand and tapped his breast pocket to check on the camera.

Traffic picked up as he approached the main commercial corridor into downtown Golden. The medical clinic was located a third of the way to town, not far from the elementary school. He'd never been to the school and never had a reason to, until today. He stepped up to a light pole and pressed the pedestrian crossing button. With a glance up the road, he could make out the mustard yellow sign of the Save Always grocery store. The color struck him as garish. He wondered if the visiting CEO might be an agent of change, as the slogan contest seemed to be important to him. If so, he'd recommend that the store's color scheme might benefit from an overhaul.

The stop signal switched to the walking man icon, so Holt stepped onto the road surface to cross. Sounds of the small town filled his senses, and he walked toward them like a man emerging from a long sleep. A local hamburger joint filled the air with the smell of charbroiled meat. He made a mental note to grill out for Mitch if he won. They would have fun with that, and it would take the pressure off Cami to cook.

He had almost made the far curb when an impatient driver rolled through the intersection, turning right on red. A car horn blared as his heel hit the curb, and he shrugged off the unnecessary warning. Over his shoulder, he caught the obscene gesture tossed out by the passing driver who grasped a long-necked amber bottle. He didn't know anyone with a white BMW, and he hadn't crossed inappropriately. He shirked it off and rounded the corner, waiting to cross the secondary road. He could have made much quicker work of this route, if only he had fixed his bicycle.

The last ten minutes of his journey passed uneventfully. He jogged into the clinic's parking lot, unable to estimate the time that had elapsed since he'd left. When he found Cami's car around back, relief that she wasn't waiting swept over him. He preferred it the other way around, as she worked and he didn't. He tied her clothes bag onto the antenna and sat down on the curb behind the car to rest his hip.

When the camera bumped against his chest, he

decided to take it out to become familiar with its focus mechanism before the assembly. Once he pressed the "on" button, the lens came to life and whirred into position. He practiced framing a bush on the corner of the building and then backed the zoom out, switching focus to Cami's clothes bag.

The sound of spinning wheels squealed from beneath her compact car's frame. Holt jumped to his feet to see what caused the commotion. The same white BMW cruised through the lot at breakneck speed. He crouched beside the car and adjusted the camera to high speed. Beyond his station, an amber bottle flew out of the driver's window and exploded across the windshield of a nearby SUV. Holt framed the culprit dead center and snapped the exposure. After waiting for the car to disappear, he stepped in front of the SUV and took another photo, this one framing the damage to the target, a wicked spider-web crack.

With glass shards everywhere, he used his shoe to scrape the amber pieces away from Cami's tires. The glass formed a makeshift pile in the empty slip between the vehicles.

A moment later Cami stood behind him, her mouth agape at the damage. "What in heaven's name happened out here?" She folded her hands across her lips.

Holt raised the camera and punched up the last two exposures.

Her expression went from questioning to accusing. "It's Bo. He's already lashing out." Cami traded the camera for the keys. She untied the bag as he unlocked the car door. A wayward shard crunched under her shoe. She stopped to study it before opening the back door. "And it looks like he's drinking. Great combination." She disappeared into the back seat and pulled the door closed.

He caught the handle and shot her a questioning look.

"You're driving so I can change back here. I assume you have a license?"

An exaggerated smile spread over his face as he got in to take the wheel. He pushed the seat back and adjusted the rearview mirror as the scrub top flew into the hatchback. A bare shoulder rose and fell from view in the mirror. "Well, now. This is going to be a ride to remember."

"Just keep your eyes on the road, Mister marketing-expert-turned-photographer."

He started the car, smiling. "I have lots of hidden attributes."

"Well, I believe I've seen a few of them," she replied. "Hey, this isn't my pink top."

"No, you'll want a solid color for the photo op, not a geometric." He caught her shocked expression in the mirror. "You can thank me later."

"Turn right, there's a back route to the school."

"Yes, ma'am. I think I like my new job. I'll call it 'Driving Miss Crazy.'" Something that resembled a sock flew into the front seat but it didn't interfere with him making his right turn. They were heading for an award assembly—if he could keep his eyes on the road.

~

Cami squirmed in her seat as the fourth grade classes filed into the school auditorium. When she bent to adjust her sandal strap, she got a closeup look at Holt's healing left calf. Her life had been caught up in a whirlwind of recovery and relationship during a relatively short time, but she wouldn't trade it for anything in the world. She straightened and focused on her guest to express her deeply felt sentiments. "Holt, I want you to know how glad I am that you're here with me."

"What? This?" He toyed with the camera settings. "You know I had to be here for the contest announcement since it gyrates in my wheelhouse."

"That part and everything together. That includes being in my life and wanting to spend time with my little family."

He slid a hand off the camera and it landed with a steady grip on her forearm. When she leaned toward him in affection, he met her halfway as though he had an important message for her. "You amaze me, and that's why I'm following you around," he whispered.

Cami puffed a loose clump of bangs out of her way and stifled the laugh his comment deserved. She had to hold back, as dignitaries now took the stage joined by the school principal.

Holt pointed to the right aisle. "Oh, there's our Mitch."

The boy turned toward the audience, so Cami stood and gave a rainbow-sized wave. He found her and shot his arms in the air, which reflected his level of excitement. She grinned at Holt as she sat back down. Soon her balled fists pressed against her sternum in anticipation. Her right knee started bouncing, and Holt's hand landed on it for a pony ride. One microphone check later, the impromptu assembly began.

~

Holt sat erect, evaluating the hierarchy of corporate manpower on the stage. The identity of the CEO was easy to discern, the most comfortable man on the platform, by far. A tall man with prominent high cheekbones and crystal gray-blue eyes fringed with bushy gray brows, he seemed genuine and approachable as he shook hands down the row of chairs. The heavyset fellow beside the CEO must have been the regional supervisor. Holt had never come in contact with him on his many trips into the store for the homeless pickups. That guy seemed all business, barely smiling even when the CEO shook his hand.

The local store manager sat in the next seat, as Holt recognized him from his portrait in the customer service area. The man stood when the CEO singled him out for attention, laughed heartily at his comments, and topped their handshake with his left hand. The CEO patted his shoulder as he sat down, obviously pleased at the interchange. Holt wondered for a brief moment what it might be like to share the workplace with a team that had synergy and respect. The thought was cut short by a smiling principal hiding a tight schedule behind her cordiality.

"Here we go." He leaned toward Cami with a wink.

She tucked a wayward hair into her ponytail and bit her tinted bottom lip.

He looked away to pretend interest in the camera setup. He couldn't allow himself to get distracted by phantom attraction at this particular moment. What had happened to his steely resolve?

~

"Good afternoon, ladies and gentlemen, girls and boys," the principal began. Cami inched forward in her seat, trying to hear. When the vice principal stepped forward and adjusted the microphone downward for her boss, she felt relieved. "I hope you can hear me better now, as we have a very exciting program today and I wouldn't want you to miss a word of it. Save Always grocery store has made its presence known in our town for as long as I can remember, but today they've given our Golden Valley students a memory to last a lifetime." Cami glanced at Holt, and he wiggled his brow at the teaser.

"Save Always generously donated all the sides for our hot dog lunch today, which included trays of assorted cookies that we managed to devour with haste." The speaker paused for laughter. "I think that is a classic tribute to what the store means to our community and how they meet our basic need to eat, with resourcefulness and respect for individual preferences. It is our sincere privilege to have the Chief Executive Officer of Save Always stores here with us this afternoon, and I am turning over the podium to him as he brings the 'best slogan competition' to its culmination. So without further delay, here is Stanley Olson, the CEO of Save Always, our corporate sponsor of the day."

The man taking the platform mesmerized Cami, a lean, tall figure in command.

Holt leaned toward her with his animated clap, a reminder to applaud the CEO's introduction. A murmur from the children sent the teachers to their feet in a futile attempt to squelch the noise. The vice principal clapped from the stage in a metered pattern.

The children echoed the disciplined clap and hushed themselves. The CEO smiled at the student section, his appreciation for their exuberance evident. Cami liked the man already, and he hadn't even opened his mouth yet.

"Thank you all so very much," Mr. Olson said. "What an absolute delight it has been for me to loosen my tie and spend the day with your students. Why, I've learned more today than fifty lectures on store management could have taught me. Let me tell you what's brimming in my heart, having listened to and talked with each class throughout the day. You and I have to start doing things a little differently—you as parents, I mean, and me as a representative of corporate America. Here's my nugget of wisdom for the day, and then we'll get to the contest results.

"We need to begin looking at our children with different eyes. We have to stop boxing them in with our prepackaged notions about the way things should be done or have been done in the past. Where's the room for innovation in that? Where's the birthing ground for the next life-changing invention or the next life-saving cure? What I learned today is that we have to unbind tomorrow and give it to them, because they are hungry for it. And even beyond their longing, tomorrow belongs to them. It's our job to offer it on the silver tray called 'today' to the very best of our abilities, and provide them a sterling platform from which to soar."

Tears welled in Cami's eyes as applause chased the CEO's words of inspiration. The students stood up and cheered, as though to accept the empowerment he offered. Holt had joined several others nearby in a standing ovation of support, but her knees proved too jelly-like to participate.

All these days of trying to keep the family together

and eking out a living suddenly wouldn't do for her anymore. And she knew why. Mitch deserved a chance to soar, not run in place until she could get her life together. She would have to give that to God, her caution and her affinity for status quo, hunkered in half a duplex under Aunt Joyce's protective umbrella. In truth, that kind of keep-it-safe treadmill existence had been tiring and impossible to maintain.

Drawing a breath, a freedom came over her, unlatched by the speaker's words and her receipt of them at a deeper level. She would brave up and give Mitch his freedom to prosper and become what God wanted him to be. She fished a tissue from her purse and dabbed the corner of her eyes, hoping to see with new clarity.

~

The CEO shuffled a paper. "I would now like to call our top five finalists to the stage."

Holt readied the camera and toyed with the settings one last time. When he looked up, Mitch already stood on stage, his hands stuffed in his pockets.

"These five students are to be commended for their outstanding efforts to put our company's purpose into the confines of a single catch-phrase." Mr. Olson clapped in the direction of the students. "Now contestants, please step forward when your name is called."

"In third place with the slogan 'My store—my window to the world' is fifth grader… Warren Inslee." The tallest boy stepped forward and the local store manager presented an oversized check for twenty-five dollars. "In second place, with the slogan 'Come hungry—come to Save Always' is third grader…

Bethany Morse." The girl squealed with delight.

Holt allowed the round of applause to hide his camera noise as he punched the lens into action. Cami's knees began bouncing again and he turned to deliver a quick wink.

"And now for the grand champion of the Save Always slogan contest with the winning slogan 'Feeding the Golden community—one day at a time' is fourth grader… Mitchell Walsh." In the exuberance of the moment, Holt managed to get the camera aligned and focused as he crouched above the crowd. Mitch let go with a super-hyped version of his victory dance, and laughter soon mixed with the applause.

The CEO helped the store manager bestow an oversized check to the winner, written for a month of free groceries. Holt clicked the shutter several times in rapid succession before Cami's arms took him hostage in personal celebration. An out-of-this-world moment, he embraced the winner's mother in the audience while Mitch shook hands with the CEO on stage. Feeling like a champion by mere association, it occurred to him that this was what being family truly felt like. If so, he had to have more, much more.

Chapter 18

Cami hesitated to go on stage but the officials had held the winners up there for pictures afterward, so she allowed Holt to lead her up the aging wooden stairs. Mitch froze for one last photo and bolted her way as soon as he spotted her. She stooped and opened her arms to catch her winner. Holt stood opposite the dignitaries and shot a few photos while Mitch showed off the huge check.

She combed the boy's cowlick down with her fingers. "Mitchell, I am so proud of you I could just bust. I held my breath the whole time until he called your name."

"Me, too." With cheeks still pink from his antics on stage, his eyes danced with excitement.

Holt approached to offer his congratulations. "Strong marketing work, Mitch." He held out his palm for a high five. The boy readily met the greeting with his slap of accomplishment, and the two collapsed in a giant hug.

Cami looked over her shoulder as the CEO regarded their little family reunion with fondness. "Hello, Mr. Olson, I'm Cami Walsh, Mitch's mother. I wanted to thank you for your nugget of wisdom to us earlier. It really struck home with me and nearly brought me to tears."

"Why, thank you so much, Mrs. Walsh. This fine young man seems ready for all the challenges life can throw at him. I am truly impressed with his work and his insight."

"Well, he might have had a little coaching in the insight department. Let me introduce you to a special friend of the family, Holt Ellis. Holt's our marketing expert."

The CEO's scrutiny sharpened. "Mr. Ellis, it's my pleasure to meet you today. You have some background in marketing, then?"

Holt shifted his weight to his strong side and seemed reluctant to answer. "Marketing was my degree discipline at UC and my career experience, but I'm unemployed at the moment and reviewing my options."

A twinkle came to the tall man's eyes. "Then how about an additional option to consider? I'm here in town to conduct interviews tomorrow for the director of our marketing department. The job starts with taking our new slogan and creating a sales campaign, incorporating its genius. I'd like to have you come in to vie for the position."

Stunned at the invitation, Holt attempted to tuck the camera in his pocket and missed.

Cami reached up, grabbed the camera, and slid it

into her back pocket. Someone stopped to take their picture and she gave Mitch a huge hug. "On   Holt's behalf, he'd be honored to, sir. Is there a certain time that works better for you?"

Holt's face blanched white in the whirlwind offering as she slid her hand in his. "Thank you so much, sir." Holt gave his head a shake. "I certainly didn't expect…"

"What? A collision of providence?" Mr. Olson asked. "I try to stay open to that kind of leading, and what I see is a family poised to make a difference for the community of Golden. Say, maybe Mitch here can give you a few pointers for your interview tomorrow. We'll see you around nine o'clock tomorrow morning." He nodded to seal the invitation.

Cami clapped her hands to her lips so no one could see her exaggerated smile. Her heart felt like it would explode.

"I'll be there and I won't disappoint you, sir." Holt extended his hand. The aging man met him halfway with the handshake, and someone snapped a photo of their pose.

Mitch landed his chubby hand on top and it became a three-way agreement that Cami couldn't resist, so she snatched her camera out. "Please hold that for me, fellas." She rushed to get the focus just right. The shutter clicked and the shot froze on her viewing screen, a scene of destiny calling right in front of her eyes.

The store manager motioned toward center stage. "Mr. Olson, we need you over here a minute." The executive bowed and departed at the man's direction.

Cami locked her arms around Holt and Mitch.

"Gentlemen, I think we'd better go celebrate with a milkshake or something." She took one step before Mitch resumed his victory dance.

Holt joined in with something akin to a hula move. "Cami, I want to grill for us tonight, so you don't have to cook." He threw his hands in the air like he didn't have a care in the world.

Cami looked at his scrape marks, top to bottom, all along his left side. A new worry emerged with a lead thump. She froze in mid-celebration and pulled his arms down. Mitch lost his waggle and landed flat-footed beside her. "Okay, Holt. Now you have a job interview tomorrow. I'm going to guess you don't have a suit to wear, do you?" His evaporating smile confirmed what she already knew. "Okay, load up and let's go." She assumed the demeanor of a drill sergeant and snapped her fingers. "We're heading straight to Goodwill to buy a suit for the next marketing director of Save Always grocery store." Holt opened his mouth as if to protest, but she cut him a matter-of-fact glance.

Mitch threw his arms open wide as though to catch them both inside a sweeping hug. "Save Always, Feeding the Golden community—one day at a time."

~

Holt contorted his face for Mitch's amusement. "This must be alien domain." Cami shot through the thrift shop door like a woman with a mission. He glanced down at what he had on, which he thought were some of his best clothes, shocked at the amount of wear they showed. This would be the day of his wardrobe's reckoning. His casual duds were done for.

Mitch parted company at a row of economy-dressed manikins. "If you need me, I'll be in the toys."

Cami tossed him a wave of permission and headed into the heart of the store.

Holt yearned to wander off as well, but he knew better than to attempt mutiny, at least not yet. He followed her down a main aisle planted like row crops, with racks of jeans, skirts, and blouses. Finally, a less pink terrain emerged—a place where his shorts matched perfectly. He recognized the land of comfortably worn, a location he was used to.

Cami forced the hangers back along the far wall. "We're in luck. They've just restocked the menswear rack. The selection's pretty good. Come on over here and let's get a feel for the right size first."

"Anything you say, Wardrobe Lady." Holt squeezed past a tie rack, squared up to the suits, and held his arms out like a hapless scarecrow.

She held up a blue polyester jacket that looked like a prep school uniform for grandpas. "Too big." She scrunched up her mouth. "That jacket is a forty-two. Guess you don't know your actual size, do you?"

The hanger hooked the rack as he watched her from behind, enjoying her intensity and her trim waistline. "M-E-D. That's my size—at least what my T-shirts tell me—but they've been known to stretch the truth."

Annoyed, Cami pummeled him with an elbow as she held up an English-looking tan jacket with suede elbow patches. She pressed the shoulder seams into the balls of his shoulders. "Hmm. Too small by at least one size." She slapped the hanger back on the rack.

He watched her skilled hands pluck through several more candidates when he spotted a color he actually favored. "How about that brown one there?" Not to be ignored, he leaned over her shoulder. "I think I like brown—not too dark because summer's coming—but earthy."

She pulled it off at his insistence, held it up to his chest, and refused to look him in the eye. "Okay, this is option number one," she replied, revealing something of a systematic approach. "I'm not sending you into the dressing room with less than three options. Got it?"

"Yes, ma'am. I'm happy to play along. How about I match this with a tie or two, then we can pick out a short sleeve shirt for each jacket?"

"Go ahead and make your selections, but if I don't like it, I'll have to be brutally honest."

"I absolutely expect as much. Hey, we're having a real Barbie-and-Ken moment, aren't we?" His hand strayed to an extra wide tie in an avant-garde print, which mesmerized him for a harmless second.

"Oh no. Absolutely no melodrama, Holt." She shoved aside the next section of suit coats. "You've met Mr. Olson. Now does he look like a man who'd admire something Picasso-like on his marketing executive?"

He dropped the tie with a shake of his head and rotated the stand until a soft yellow tie with tiny gray diamonds appeared. He pulled it off the knob and laced it across the brown jacket, formulating his opinion. If possession was truly nine-tenths of the law, maybe she'd let him have it if he held onto it long enough.

"Let's try a navy combination." Cami layered a second suit over the first.

He turned back to the tie rack and found a plain gray tie that was too shiny for his taste but would do on short notice.

Cami dangled a black pinstripe suit in her fingers

as her final selection. "I think we're ready to hit the shirt rack."

Holt opened his mouth to object and then thought better of it. The shirt rack proved to be half the length of a football field with no rhyme or reason to it. Holt tried to navigate along its length to help Cami identify some worthy options but felt like a moving coat rack with his triple load. Out of nowhere, a blue apron-clad teenager rolled a shopping cart up to him and left it with a smile. He poured his future wardrobe into the cart's belly and flexed his biceps to regain feeling in his arms. Cami had two shirts in hand by then, one white and one gray. He spotted a light brown shirt with faint stripes and plopped the yellow tie against it for matching purposes.

"Too much going on there." Cami glanced up to slice the brown combination with her disdain, and then moved on down the rack.

"Maybe not." He redeemed the shirt and added it to the realm of possibilities.

"Okay, let's go with this batch for now." She folded her selections over the cart rim. "Off to the dressing room with you. I'm heading over to men's shoes after I check on Mitch. I'll be back for inspection. I want to see you in each of the suits."

"I bet you do, as this is a voyeur's picnic right here," he teased. When she volleyed back with a short-tempered look, Holt took the shopping cart into full retreat until a mirrored stall fell open on his left. Digging down to retrieve the brown option, he decided to show her a thing or two, right off the bat. The yellow tie trailed him into the stall like Eeyore's prone-to-wander tail, only it wasn't buttoned in its proper place yet.

~

Cami stood outside the dressing room door, ready for the process to shape up a bit. Tomorrow's interview was too important to screw up with the wrong look. She would make sure that didn't happen. "Come out and let me have a look at you."

A shuffle of footwork occurred under the stall door as Holt stuffed his feet into a pair of dress shoes. He threw the latch and the door fell open revealing nothing—until he stepped out from behind the side panel in pure GQ style. He took a few exaggerated steps pretending to be a male model and then unbuttoned his jacket with a flip of his wrist.

She had to spread her feet apart as appreciative astonishment washed over her like a rogue wave. "Good glory garden peas," she muttered under her breath, unable to look away. "Walk around a bit more to give the shoes a workout."

He made a few basketball moves and pulled up for a jump shot. The brown-on-brown combination did something inexplicable for him, as his facial features seemed highlighted all the more. And his eyes matched the center of the tiny diamonds on his tie. The more she studied him, the more liquid she turned inside. "Be sure about those shoes. Try on another pair to see what works best." She attempted to regain her composure with a deep breath. "And let's pick out a second shirt, in case you get a call-back interview."

"You're being generous, but I want you to know that I'm considering this an advance loan off my first paycheck." He backed toward the changing stall.

She read the raw sincerity in his eyes and nodded

as his smile lassoed her back from the visual slaying she'd just encountered. "It's never going to be about the money, Holt." Her voice sounded husky and she watched it register on his face.

"No, it's about being there for each other." He closed the stall door with a wink.

Cami reached for the rejected suits to return them to the rack.

Mitch ran up the aisle. "Where's Holt?"

Cami cleared her throat to reply but never got a squeak out.

"In here, buddy. What's up?"

"They've got a really awesome bike back here. No kidding, you've really gotta see it," the boy gushed.

Cami hooked the ties on the round rack and shoved the suits back in place, intent to keep the damage to her spending budget reined in. "Oh, no you don't." Her protest came out a little louder than intended. "We've got to stay focused on the task at hand." Mitch's face deflated as a pair of shoes sailed under the stall door.

"Come on, now," Holt replied. "It never hurt anything to have a look."

The boy grabbed the shoes and clapped them together, disappearing down the aisle.

Cami put the extra shirts back and strolled toward the dressing room.

Holt exited, his intended purchases neatly folded across his arm and the shoes tucked under his elbow. He nodded toward a sales flyer on the mirror. "Pink tags are half off today. That makes my suit a total of four dollars."

"You're a cheap date, Ken—even for the prom." She took possession of the suit, shirt, and shoes.

"If only we were done shopping, my dear Barbie." He headed straight for the back of the store where Mitch had disappeared.

Cami lost track of him as he turned behind the multi-level shoe display, but soon heard his whoop of exclamation. "What on earth could this be?" She rounded the corner at a cautious speed. There along the aisle sat her two men perched on a bicycle-built-for-two. She covered her mouth in genuine shock. Mitch pedaled from the front without effect as the chain had slouched off the sprocket, but Holt's face fully arrested her gaze. His sad puppy eyes stared imploringly at her. The longer she maintained eye contact, the more she came unglued. "What in the world would we do with this monstrosity?" She began to feel ludicrous for even considering it.

"We could deliver food to the homeless together," Mitch replied, earning him a high-five from Holt. Their pedaling fell into synchrony on their mock trip around the homeless loop.

"Well, how much would this extra purchase set me back?" She had to ask, still split on the decision and at war with her pragmatic side.

"Twenty-five dollars," Holt replied, "on loan from Bicycle Man, of course."

Mitch flew off the bike seat to wrap her in a pre-deal hug.

Holt slid off to commandeer the handlebars, bringing the bicycle up the aisle.

In surrender, Cami did the mental math to make sure they had enough money. "Okay, guys. I double-dog dare anybody to make me regret this ridiculous impulse purchase even for one minute." She refused to look at them again. She grabbed the shopping cart and followed Holt up the aisle. In the throes of victory, her companions yipped like feral dogs all the way to the register. She truly wanted a reason to celebrate, half-filled with expectation of what tomorrow might bring. But today, dread still ruled and made her reluctant to open her purse.

Chapter 19

Holt leaned back on the glider with his eyes closed to reflect on the day's cascading events. Mitch had won the slogan contest, tumbling him into position for the job interview of a lifetime. He'd somehow come home with a new look and a new bicycle-steed, quite the icon of forward motion. The smell of flame-kissed burgers still lingered over the patio as he had treated Mitch to a hero's dinner. Cami had coached him through some last-minute changes on his resume and then printed it out for the interview. With the night growing late, Mitch was receiving his bedtime ritual to cap their big day. Sleep sounded like a prime option. He may have actually dozed off for a few seconds, as the glider had come to a standstill beneath him.

The screen panel slid on its tracks and Cami emerged, looking comfortable and bearing the candle, which had started to burn low in the jar. She wiggled in beside him and put her head on his shoulder. The smell of powder soon permeated the air. "Let's practice the interview." She leaned toward him and he kissed her hair for the go-ahead. "As a candidate, how are you well-matched for promoting this company?"

He let the question swirl around until it picked up some related thoughts. "I sense the importance of the grocer's role in the life of the community—the connection that comes from its provision—possibly even to a point of co-dependency. That's an asset, not something either party should take advantage of. It's much more appropriate that we respect our mutual roles. Our marketing should echo that kind of respect."

"Good, I like that respect part. Be sure you get that communicated."

"Okay coach, fire off another one." He pushed the glider and waited for the volley.

"What would you say your greatest strengths are?"

He smiled, knowing this was standard interview fodder, but it pleased him to keep their exchange going. "My organizational skills are a strength for the marketing position. I also multitask well, follow up projects with due attention, and strongly honor deadlines. One of my core values is doing my best, which makes me strive harder to get my work accomplished and do a superior job."

A pause seeped between them as Cami filtered his response in preparation for the next area of investigation. "What if I think you have another outstanding quality that might trump all of that other good stuff?"

"Exactly what would that be, in your humble-but-accurate opinion?"

She shifted away from him, down to the glider's end. She brought her knees up to her chest and kneaded her toes under his thigh. "Your people skills are your best attribute, Holt. I think Mr. Olson should hear that from you. He's building his team to ensure success for the company, and you're the quintessential connector. He'd expect that from his marketing department. You're the one candidate that can deliver it."

He took her feet in his hands, giving her comments some thought. "Wouldn't it seem too much like bragging if I went spouting off about being a people-person? I'm uncomfortable enough focusing on myself so much during the interview. Help me find a balance here." When her right foot flexed, he traced her arch with his thumb.

"Maybe you could say, 'I've been told that I have good people skills and I find strong personal fulfillment in face-to-face interactions.'"

"Yeah, even if all I get sometimes is feet with fancy toenails, I enjoy the interaction." She gave a defiant little kick but he wasn't going to let that break his connection with her.

"Okay. Here's my next question then. If you were asked to fire off your top two or three brainstorming ideas for Save Always, what would they be?"

"The very first thing I would initiate is a sweeping update of the company logo and signage. Right now, it's glaringly outdated—a remnant from the seventies."

"That criticism comes from a man who wants to ride a tandem bicycle around town?"

He lunged at her with one arm and attempted to pull Cami toward him.

She resisted with a laugh. "What else can you come up with?"

"Well, my food-for-work program is high priority for me, so I'd like to see some integration of caring for the community woven into the company's image fairly rapidly."

"That jobs program is certainly in the realm of the unexplored. And Save Always is already involved in some of that, donating expired food to the homeless."

"Food credit accounts would raise the stakes a bit, but it would also generate a new customer base as someone would be paying for the food. I trust that would appeal to Mr. Olson's business sense, plus lend the company additional goodwill in the community. That's another thing I would tout—everything the company already does for the people of Golden."

"Like making recycle bins available?"

"Exactly. They also have some kind of teacher award every year, don't they?"

"Yeah, it's called the Golden Apple award. And they donate cookie trays for special events in the community. They sent some to us at the grand opening of the clinic."

"Package all of these individual offerings together and give the administrators strokes for what they're doing right."

"And then help them update the rest. Holt, I think you're on fire for this position. Just let that passion show, and you're in."

"Any more questions?" His tone teased, but not his glance down the glider.

"Well, what are your weaknesses? We didn't get to that one."

He gave her a throaty protest as he lunged, caught her, and pulled her to his side. "You are my weakness," he whispered. The next wordless interlude melted into her full approval of his confession with only the stars as witness overhead.

~

"Mitch, it's time to get out to the bus stop, honey." Cami snagged her keys from the desk. "Holt, we need to leave or I'll be late for work."

"Right here raring to go." He threw a fistful of food into the cat's bowl and lowered it onto the floor. "Do you have my resume?"

"There on the counter in the manila envelope."

"What about a legal pad for me to jot down my ideas?"

Cami pointed to the end cabinet. "Bottom drawer." She hit the front door latch and released Mitch to catch the bus at a run. "I have ink pens in the car, Holt. Let's roll." A creature of habit, she dove into the driver's seat and started the engine. He pulled the front door closed and checked the lock, then quick-stepped to the passenger's side.

"Right. You drive and I'll pray." He brushed some cat hair from his lapel, and then grabbed his seat belt.

Cami glanced down. The wrinkles in her scrubs would make an elephant's hide look ironed, and her nerves sat on edge. She backed down the driveway in haste and wheeled the car onto the road.

Holt bowed his head but kept his eyes open. "Lord, this is your day. Help it be one that we'll feel your remarkable presence in. Thank you for this job interview and all the mutual support to get me prepared. Lord—if it's in your will and part of how you want to bless me—please let me land this job. And watch over all of us today. In Jesus' name, amen."

Cami floored the accelerator and turned left against traffic, pressing her passenger against the seat back. "Good thing you got the 'watch over all of us' part out." She checked her rearview mirror for any fallout.

Holt cleared his throat and fingered the resume pack like it contained arsenic. "I need some serious input for a second." He attempted to straighten his yellow tie and the resume slid from his lap.

Her face turned to stone as she wondered what kind of complication he was whipping up next. "Go ahead, I guess."

"I want to have an honest answer when Mr. Olson asks me about my relationship with you. Any suggestions?"

"I think I introduced you as a family friend. What's wrong with that?"

"That's not enough for me—and not honest enough for my heart." He stared at her. "I'd like to say that you're my girlfriend, Cami. How do you feel about that?"

She wasn't sure she'd even heard the question correctly, as her heart had begun pounding in her ears. Suddenly the steering wheel seemed to sweat under her hands and the sun had not even come up good yet. She searched for a reply and said the first thing that made any sense. "I don't know about 'girlfriend.' It sounds a little teenager-ish." She veered right to catch the next light. "Maybe you should aim for keeping it professional today. Let him read between the lines if he wants to."

Holt placed his hand on her forearm in sincerity. "I

hope you're not hedging for some inexplicable reason."

Cami tried to swallow but the steam traveling up her neck made it nearly impossible. "Look, I think falling in love is personal." She tried not to sound agitated. "No one should expect you to convey that as part of a job interview, for pity's sake."

"Okay, I'll fight my way out of that corner if I get backed into it. What's more important is that you and I can be genuine with each other about what's going on."

She glanced at the green light, hooked a left and sent a questioning look his way. "You don't think I'm being genuine?" Her brow knit with emotion.

He looked at her as if she was speaking a foreign language.   "I want you to be my girlfriend and I'm prepared to shout it from the mountaintop." He motioned to the distant ridge filling the windshield.

Cami glanced at the clock on the dashboard, which wouldn't hold onto the six o'clock hour much longer. She white-knuckled the car into the clinic's back lot and literally jumped out at a run. "Good luck with the job interview, Holt." She fumed her way across the parking lot. Why he had to go and hoist that mountain up at her this morning, she'd never know. Relief filled her lungs as she pulled the clinic's door open to disappear inside. Sure, the people here were needy, too, but only in a medical way.

~

Holt sat in the café area of Save Always, comfortable yet circumspect. He reviewed his notes and sketches as early-bird grocery shoppers trickled by. He had developed a three-pronged plan to kick off the new marketing initiative, which included a new company logo with Mitch's slogan at the forefront. His thoughts digressed to the confusing conversation with Cami, wondering if it was only a last minute case of nerves. He tucked the resume envelope under the notepad and leaned back to enjoy the yeast-led aromas wafting from the bakery.

Mr. Olson appeared at the far end of the counter and began to make small talk with Holt's old friend Julie, the bakery manager. Her warm laugh rippled across the room, and he felt blessed in the moment. In a blink, the CEO headed his way with two cups of coffee.

"Good morning, Holt. Glad you could make it."

Holt stood to greet his host. "Thank you for inviting me, Mr. Olson."

"Right this minute I'm just plain old Stan." He handed the coffee to him. "How's my friend Mitch this morning?"

"Well, by the time I got over there, he was busting through the front door and running full-tilt for the bus."

"There's certainly a corporate lesson to be learned there." He chuckled before taking a sip.

Holt grabbed a sugar packet and began to doctor his steaming brew. With two stirs it became drinkable.

"I appreciate you being here early. It gives me a chance to get to know you better before the formal part begins. For starters, tell me about your walk through the valley of unemployment. I know it hasn't been an easy economy for young professionals to build a career on."

"No, sir. It hasn't been. Once I was laid off from my full-time job in Denver, I decided that I'd rather be part time in Golden than anywhere else, so I tethered myself here and took odd jobs in and around marketing to keep a roof over my head."

"Hard times are enough to shake a man to his core.

What kept you motivated, if you don't mind me asking?"

"My faith, mostly." Holt relaxed, enjoying the warmth that radiated from the cup. "I wonder if God puts a holding pattern on that will-work-for-food phase to keep us humble and dependent. I lost a lot of material things during that period, but I never lost my faith in God." Somehow that disclosure had an element of satisfaction to it, and he straightened his posture.

"When did the pretty lady and her clever son enter the picture?"

"Only a few weeks back, when I decided to come down the mountain without my bicycle fully under me. That run-in was divinely orchestrated." Holt glanced down at the swirl inside his cup. "She's been a big part of my recuperation on several fronts, especially since she's a nurse."

"And a sharp-looking nurse, too." The aging man leaned toward him. "I married a nurse myself. It was the best move I've ever made."

Holt shared the conspirator's moment and leaned in to narrow the gap between them. "I'm certifiably head-over-heels, if we can keep that off the record." His smile animated. "I'm living next door, housesitting for her aunt over the summer. That makes me the duplex handyman and lets me help Cami keep an eye on Mitch."

"Bravo for being a strong male influence for him. So many kids don't have that type of role model nowadays. I figured you might have coached him a little with the marketing slogan, which is partly why I've asked you to come in today. Now, don't be too hard on the young whippersnappers competing against you for the position. Granted, they're a little wet behind the ears." A twinkle shone in his eyes. The next instant, his tall frame unfolded and he pushed back the chair to depart.

Holt fought the urge to stand but he did take the hand being offered across the table. "I'll bring my best game into the interview. We'll see if they can keep up."

"You do that. I'll see you at nine o'clock in the general manager's office right behind Customer Service."

"Looking forward to it, sir." Holt watched in anticipation as the man strolled away. Before he knew it, an apple-topped pastry appeared in front of him. He looked up to find the bakery manager shuffling back to her workspace.

"You're a blessing, Julie." He fingered the crescent-shaped treat while his mouth watered.

"Look who's talking," she replied, pulling her apron strings into a bow behind her back.

Holt took the first flaky bite and allowed the blessing of his happenstance encounter with the CEO to fan the flames of his motivation to land the job. He didn't want to leave the store without its guarantee—a food-share plan of a higher sort, called regular income.

Chapter 20

Cami attempted to read three throat cultures incubating at the nurse's station. In a rush to organize her paperwork, she fumbled a box of paperclips and its contents showered across the countertop.

Doctor Harrison glanced up, his brow knit. "Judge Stallings plans to add vehicle vandalism to the claims against Bo. Is something getting your goat this morning, Nurse Walsh?"

"Oh, Holt and I had a conversation that ran afoul on the way in this morning. He's interviewing for a marketing job with Save Always right now and I guess I'm a little tense, that's all." She picked at the errant clips like a chicken pecking the dirt.

"Well, I'm sure he's more than qualified." He corralled a few loose mavericks and pushed them back toward the box. "For your part, you need to have a mustard seed of faith that he'll represent himself in the best possible light during the interview process."

She winced as if the truth had jabbed her under the ribs. "The issue of how he represents *me* is what has become problematic."

"Aha! That's a horse of a different color, indeed." The doctor leaned closer. "May I say that I've noticed a bit more radiance in your pleasant demeanor lately? I must admit, this gentleman seems to be good medicine for you."

"I certainly feel it—but I'm having a hard time expressing it, I guess. I'm not used to this co-dependence thing, and it scares me in quiet moments, if I let myself overthink it."

His chuckle started deep in his throat. "What's truly scary is a life without it. By the way, all three of your cultures are negative. I'll take it from here."

"Thank you, Doctor Harrison—for your words of wisdom this morning."

"Remember that being in love doesn't mean leaping off a cliff. Try nurturing it one baby step at a time. You might be amazed where it can take you."

"If my heart could just dialogue with my feet, I'd be much more willing to go."

"Atta-girl! Now answer that page to room three like my best nurse, will you?"

She smiled and stuffed the paperclips into the confines of their small box where they could be happy without her. After a deep sigh, she resigned herself to duty and gave the heart-check a postponement.

~

Holt had completed three-quarters of the second exercise of the morning, a situational ethics evaluation that made him dig deep into his vault of experience to provide actual examples. He leaned back to cross his ankles between questions and noticed a huddle of executives that seemed to be gaining noisy momentum up front. He wondered what the point of sudden interest could have been and rubbed his eyes to wipe away the blur from the fine print.

Mr. Olson nodded several times during the discussion and handed part of what appeared to be someone's resume to the general manager. The round-faced man glanced up at Holt, making definite eye contact with him before surrendering the page and offering his input. Holt squelched a funny feeling the exchange birthed. He could only hope that the upper-level discussion could advance in his favor, as the four young professionals seated behind him had been nipping at his heels all morning.

The next question regarded any career regrets that he might have, either in his educational training or his work experience. Cami's emphasis on his people-connecting skills came to mind so he decided to build an answer off that claim, pinpointing his lack of training in social work, which could have benefitted his interaction with the homeless in the community. He finished composing the response and then read back through it, hoping to make it come across as positive as possible—for a regret.

"Time's up, gentlemen," the manager said with a glance at the clock. "I need to collect your questionnaires at this time. Mr. Olson is ready to conduct the individual interviews next, so we'll start alphabetically. Holt Ellis, you'll go first. Mr. Olson is waiting in my office, to the left of Customer Service."

"Thank you, sir." Holt handed in his questionnaire. The manager squeezed out a compressed smile and seemed off-balance, as if something pending hung in the air. It occurred to him that he might as well have been thanking the guard standing beside the guillotine, as this procession now took on the dead counterweight of candidate elimination. He ran his fingers through his hair and somehow remembered to button his jacket on the way in.

~

Cami escorted the budding skateboard pro to the x-ray lab. Her mind wandered as she went. The patient lagged behind since he walked with a considerable limp. Focused beyond the clinic, she wondered how far along Holt might be in the interview process, and whether the topic of their relationship had surfaced. Dread perched on her chest at the mere thought, and she acknowledged that the issue deserved some further introspection. She turned to check her patient's progress and caught him peeking into the break room.

"Hey, sorry about my speedy pace," she said. "Have you eaten yet this morning, by any chance?"

His curly mop shook in response, his eyes hollow.

Cami detoured straight to the refrigerator and retrieved her lunch sack. She pulled out leftovers from last night's grill and popped it into the microwave. Next she fished a bottle of water out of the overhead cabinet and put it all on a cafeteria tray. When the microwave dinged, she pulled the burger out and centered it between the fruit and chips. "Let's take this down to x-ray with us, since they usually have us wait a spell." He didn't say a word, but she did catch him eyeing the cheeseburger. For a fleeting second, she related to

Holt's reward for feeding the hungry and claimed the teeny warm fuzzy it produced in her heart.

~

"Holt Ellis." The CEO read from the top of his resume. He lowered the paper and gave him a questioning look. "Or should I call you Bicycle Man?"

Holt tensed in his chair, unable to hide his shock at the disclosure. Even with his thorough practice session, he had not anticipated such an exposing turn of events. "I go by both, sir, depending on the setting." He tried to read the man's expression amid his own confused thoughts. "May I ask how you found out?"

Mr. Olson nodded in silent compliance and leafed through Holt's resume. In seconds he produced the last page, the newspaper article taped to copy paper.

The piercing truth became apparent. Cami had set him up without even consulting him. The marketing expert battled with the people-person side of him as his emotions teetered between anger and apprehension.

"I found this in your application and it sure snagged my attention."

"Mr. Olson, you'll have to excuse me. I had no idea that feature article had been included in my resume packet." His confession came across weak, and his voice, strained.

"Apparently not," the CEO replied. "This brings us both to a rather unique juncture, wouldn't you say?"

"Sir, I feel like I need to apologize for the apparent dichotomy, as you were looking for a marketing professional…"

"And I got an advocate for the homeless. Is that what you mean?" He sat back in the executive chair, his fingertips pressed into a teepee that hovered above his lips. "Well, well. Never in a hundred years." The exclamation came muttered under his breath as if he couldn't prevent it.

Holt fought the stab he felt in his gut as any hope he had for the position began to leak out of his once-high spirits. Attempting to staunch his losses, he slid forward in his chair, desperate to make things right. "Sir, tell me what I can say to you to earn your trust back." Somehow Joyce's voice echoed into memory, reminding him that honesty always proved the best policy. "Let me be candid with you. I am both men. Marketing is my professional career, and serving the homeless is my charitable calling. One doesn't diminish the other, and they both make me who I am."

"I'll tell you what you can say, Holt Ellis, a.k.a. Bicycle Man." The CEO lowered the teepee and braced forward on his elbows. "Say that you will take this marketing director position with Save Always, not just because I am offering it to you right now since you're by far the most qualified candidate, but because of what it will mean to our company to have you on board as staff." A sincere smile followed the offer across the table.

Holt tilted his head, not even sure he had heard the man correctly. His solo interview had barely begun, plus four young men in the other room waited their turn to pitch for the position. Fighting back the numbness of disbelief, he swiped a hand across his face.

The CEO leaned closer still, his eyes now sparkling. "Maybe I should explain the 'never in a hundred years' part of what I said earlier. In the cloudy morass called the back of my mind, I've been trying to figure out how to achieve a more community-linked image for our company. Yes, I want us, in the long-term, to be both profitable and a business success. That's something my father ingrained in me back in the seventies. But of increasing importance to me as I grow older, I want to look back on my life's work at Save Always and see the positive impact we've had within the communities our stores serve."

Buoyed, Holt began to glimpse some daylight for his future direction. "The bottom line is always more than dollars and cents, sir."

"Of course it is, but up until this day I haven't been able to figure out how to pull it all together. Today, the solution to accomplishing that goal is finally sitting right in front of me."

"I'm honored that you would even think that, sir—honored beyond belief." Holt rested one hand on the edge of the desk. "I've sketched out a draft proposal on how to get started with a revamp of our image, starting with Mitch's winning slogan."

"Wait a minute, son. You just said 'our image.' Does that mean you'll accept the job?"

A wave of gratitude hit Holt, bringing him to his feet. "Why yes, sir. Whatever job you're offering me, I want it." He bridged the gap over the desktop with his right arm and the CEO clasped his hand to pump it vigorously.

The store's general manager opened the office door and peered in, seeking direction.

"Send those other gentlemen home, Henry. I believe I have my man right here."

The door closed, leaving Holt alone with his new employer, as giddy elation began to tickle his sternum. Under God's favor, he had achieved his career's comeback at last.

Mr. Olson locked his gaze on him, eyes shining. "I'm thinking to rename the position Marketing and Community Relations Director. How does that sound to you?"

"Like a dream come true, sir. Honestly—both of my passions united in one job."

"Never in a hundred years." The CEO's rising tone echoed his culminating pleasure.

It occurred to Holt that time proved inconsequential when God intended to lavish a blessing. His divine nature somehow operated outside of time, which made the blessing all the sweeter when it did eventually land. He pulled in a breath. It felt good to be alive.

"Now how about we have a look at that revamping proposal? I'm only in town until two o'clock, but I'm all ears until then. Let's leave the nitty-gritty employment paperwork for Henry later, shall we?"

Holt shifted his chair forward with a nod and laid the updated logo sketch on the desktop. He knew he could be an asset to Save Always and be fully blessed at the same time. Never had a first step felt so good.

~

Cami sat down with her substitute lunch and tried to block out the noises around her. After a numbing eight-year wait, things now cascaded in rapid succession. Caught in the torrent, her heart floated forward but her mind still dragged an anchor. Why had she blown up at Holt just because he wanted to call her his girlfriend? Clearly, courtship remained uncharted waters for her, one she navigated through like a real landlubber.

She nibbled at the peanut butter cracker and reflected on Holt's visit to her church. He'd made a specific prayer request for a job. Now, miraculously, a mere two days later, he interviewed for an incredible position with Save Always. Mitch flitted to mind as she realized how special Holt treated her son and genuinely cared about them both. So what was her problem? Didn't she want a relationship like that? Sure, she'd been praying for one, hope-against-hope.

The last thought made her flinch as she reached for another cracker. Maybe she never expected God to care enough to answer her ongoing prayer, like the mountains somehow blocked her requests. And now that God had brought Holt into her life, she managed to drag her feet. Wasn't her faith more real than that?

The cracker turned into mush inside her mouth and she took a long drink from the water bottle. There was only one thing she could do to make things right. She had to apologize, first to God and then to Holt.

"Bleeder in room three," Doctor Harrison said through the doorway. "Sorry to cut your lunch short."

She popped to her feet, responding to duty. "I wouldn't call this lunch anyway." Her cell phone vibrated as she rounded the doorway and she took the call on the move. "Ms. Walsh, it's Tammy from school. Mitch's father is here in the office wanting to check him out for lunch today, but I don't see anyone else listed on our authorization sheet."

Cami hesitated with the complication but knew she had mere seconds to deal with this personal matter and get back to work, as a bleeding patient waited in room three.

"Have him give his name and I'll let you know if

it's okay, Tammy." The ensuing pause ate away at Cami's patience as she had more than one open wound to attend.

"Holt Ellis is here. Should I release Mitch then?" Tammy's level tone reflected a professional demeanor.

"Yes. You've got my permission. And tell them to have fun at lunch." The phone slid back into Cami's pocket as her shoulder pushed the door open and met another hardship case.

~

Holt sat across from Stan Olson and savored the meatloaf plate that had been presented him by the deli staff. The café area pulsed with activity. Mothers brought their children in for midday treats, as the deli had a reputation for fun and inexpensive baked goods, thanks to Julie. He enjoyed the distraction of their noisy antics.

"The only way I've figured out how to keep any quality control for our deli is to submit my taste buds to the product directly." Stan stirred a lump of semi-congealed brown gravy into his potatoes.

Holt hesitated before picking up his fork and looked at the man's sincere face. "Would it be okay for me to bless the food before you analyze it, sir?" He folded his napkin into his lap.

His lunch date smiled and retired his fork early, then nodded and closed his eyes. The children produced a solar flare of ambient noise.

Holt grinned and closed his eyes. "Father, we thank you for the provision of food today and for our business to bring it to your children in a fair and cost effective manner. Help us be good stewards of everything you've entrusted to us, in the name of Jesus we pray, amen."

"I appreciate a man who doesn't hide his faith, Holt. That will serve you well in the long run. Back when I started, we kept faith bottled up and contained within the church walls. Thank goodness we live under grace and learned how to 'let it all hang out,' as the hippies used to say."

"I've always held that flower power and peace belonged to God first anyway." His joking tone soon muffled into a creamy starch load. He savored the salty sensation. When the yellow tie tried to halt his first swallow, he loosened the knot, under his new boss' full inspection.

"Something tells me we're going to get along like bookends." Stan tugged his tie off and stuffed it in his breast pocket. "Keeps the food stains off." He patted the protection compartment.

Holt wiped his hands and mirrored the wardrobe treatment, enjoying his new freedom and the unanticipated friendship it ushered in.

~

Cami's bleeder turned out to be a frail little lady in her mideighties. She prepped the deep cut on the base of her thumb and washed all the encrusted blood away.

The patient's elderly husband clucked his tongue at the grave situation. "Making ham sandwiches for lunch, she was." His lament echoed unanswered across the exam room. "We've been married nearly sixty years now, would have been more if she hadn't played so hard to get."

When the woman moaned, Cami gave her a wry smile. Dabbing the area dry with cotton gauze, she focused on the deep, half-inch cut. She brought the tube of skin glue into proximity. With its tip, she traced a thin line over the knife's destructive path and offered a silent prayer that it would hold. When she glanced at her patient, the woman had turned a whiter shade of pale. Maybe some distraction would help.

Cami performed a one-handed cleanup around the exam bed, ever holding the injured thumb above the patient's heart level. "Mrs. Clemmons, can I ask you for some advice, woman-to-woman?" Once the patient nodded, she cleared her throat to loosen the revelation. "Lately I've been finding life in the valley has a sweetness to it, mainly because I'm falling in love for the first time. But my problem is, I look up to those brooding mountains and hesitate, like they have me hemmed in so I can't see the future. Do you have any advice to offer me?" She tossed the bloody cotton wad toward the biowaste disposal slot and it slid right in.

"Mercy, honey. Those brooding mountains have never helped a soul. It's their creator who you can trust to help you." The woman's words came life-tested, slow and deliberate.

"He who never sleeps or slumbers will watch you when you do," Mr. Clemmons replied, his eyes closed in reverence.

The quote struck Cami more like a poem than scripture, but it could have been both. She never thought about the mountains being an insignificant barrier to Almighty God. Somehow, the memory verse about making the mountain move by possessing a tiny seed of faith gained a foothold inside her heart. By similar coincidence, the glue job set and held.

Chapter 21

The pressure of nursing responsibilities shed off her shoulders as Cami exited the medical center. Now she had the privilege of playing worthy girlfriend and mother, both of which she fully longed to be. Neither Holt nor her car was anywhere to be seen, so she headed for a shady spot under a blooming mimosa tree. Her stomach growled in protest of her light lunch, but the emptiness somehow made her feel closer to God, as though she had fasted to gain insight. Under an arching branch full of pink pom-pom blooms, she drew a cleansing breath and began to whisper a prayer for direction. Before she could clamp amen onto the prayer, her car appeared at the far drive.

She stepped out into the clear so Holt would spot her, not that her white scrubs didn't stand out from the scenery like a misplaced snowman. The thought of being near him brought a heated blush up her neck, and, for the first time, she didn't fight the feeling. When the car angled over, she stepped toward the passenger door and pulled it open. A blinding bouquet of mixed flowers met her, the stargazer lily in its center an absolute knockout.

"Are these for me?" She reached for them, unable to hide her astonishment.

The driver nodded and retracted the bouquet to lure her in. "From me but strongly advised by our good friend Mr. Olson." Holt leaned toward her as if to hypnotize her further but she stiff-armed him back across the console and shut the door.

She jabbed her thumb to the right. "Head for the little park around the corner. Let's catch up with each other's days somewhere more romantic that the clinic's back lot."

He replied with a throaty hum that seemed to start deep in his chest only to be delivered through parted lips.

Cami forced her gaze ahead until she could make out the carved wooden sign announcing the tiny park. Once he nosed the car in, she jumped out and headed for a large fir tree that hung its majestic branches in a conical skirt brushing the ground.

Within seconds, Holt stepped close, the flowers cradled in the crook of his arm. "You go first." A dimple popped up to mark his pleasure.

Her heart skipped a beat. "Okay, first off, I apologize for being difficult this morning. I should have been honored that you'd want to mention me at all. I've regretted my reaction most of the day, and I beg you to forgive me."

A smile spread across Holt's face. "You're

forgiven in full. You might be interested to know you were the first thing we talked about. Mr. Olson approached me this morning in the café before the formal interview and we had a nice, private chat over coffee about several personal matters."

Surprise surged through her but she leveled the shock wave out with a steady flow of admiration. "See, you were right to address the issue, and intuitive, too." She touched his elbow and his smile hooked toward his other cheek. A pair of sparrows flitted into the tree canopy and chirped happily from a nearby branch. She pulled him into step and they began to walk, arm-in-arm, along the jogging trail. "I've had to pray through some things today, although the clinic's pace didn't allow me much in-between time."

He bumped her shoulder with his. "Do you mean about us?"

Noticing the nearness of his scratched side, she traced her fingertips along his collarbone, wishing the external damage would all heal up and go away. Determined to make that part of her prayer for him, she committed herself at that moment. "Yes, mostly about us." She squared up to look him right in the eyes. "Doctor Harrison gave me some good advice on taking it one step at a time, and I even had patients lending me some of their wisdom, especially an elderly couple that helped me gain new perspective. In short, I want you to know that you've touched my heart in a special way from the first day we met. There's certainly no getting around that this has been a one-of-a-kind encounter from the start."

He pulled her closer. "Well, maybe all that pain was worth my grand entrance, then."

She gave his scraped cheek a tender peck, but resumed the walk to buy time for her full confession. "In the dark of the evening while you held me in your arms, the relationship seemed delightfully easy. Those evenings together gave me the first real companionship I've ever had in my adult life. They came like medicine to a sick and lonely woman."

"Our nights together are my favorite, too. It levels out the rest of the day, no matter what might have gone right or wrong."

The mutual honesty of his admission caused the blush to pulse up her neck again. Needing some quick camouflage, she plucked the bouquet from his grasp and tucked it under her chin. His approval radiated from his expression, and she choked back the bashful sensation, wanting to continue. "I think I was okay with every aspect of our relationship until it came time to label it. That's when my classic foot dragging began. What does that tell you about a person who's willing to live the thrill but afraid to call it what it is?"

"Maybe it says she's had to live cautiously for too long and doesn't know how to let go and trust God for certain matters of the heart." He drew her into the shade of a cluster of small oaks. He faced around and looked deep into her eyes. "There's always a right time to let go."

"And today, I fully let go and let God bless me with this wonderful friendship." She snuggled against him and a buzz radiated through her head that even drowned out the bird chatter. "I'm not afraid to move forward, Holt. You can call me your girlfriend or whatever you want. You have my heart and I'm yours."

He touched her hair, his gray-blue eyes sparkling

as he seemed to restrain himself to prolong the moment. A bird flew by and gave a call on the wing.

She peered up at him over an arching brow. "Would you like to say anything?"

"Only that I don't feel as though I can call you my girlfriend for much longer than the duration of this summer, what with Aunt Joyce coming back to claim her turf and all." He shuffled the toe of his dress shoe in the dirt. "As the new director of marketing and community relations for Save Always, it might help my position if I settled down and became a family man in the near future."

Her hands collapsed over her mouth and her delight squealed right through her fingers. An explosion of pride detonated inside her chest.

Holt dutifully caught the flower bouquet before it found the dirt and rose with a smile. "I've been meaning to tell you the interview outcome all this time, but you seemed in a rush to say something more important."

"Well, my part of the conversation ends right now." She moved into intimate range. "Except for my last comment, which I've been thinking about half the afternoon." When Holt lifted the flowers with a questioning look, Cami grabbed his slackened necktie and leveraged him toward her until they met right at lip level. Wrapped in love, she lingered under the scent of fresh-cut flowers and the touch of a regenerated man. Under the influence of attraction, she gave in to a second breathless kiss, lending the birds something to chirp about. She drew back from his mesmerizing spell and glimpsed the double set of dimples she'd been longing to witness.

~

Holt had never experienced such wholeness as they headed through the entrance to the duplex. He had a job, a future, and a woman who loved him to tie it all together. Definitely standing in God's splash zone for showers of blessings, the effect was amazing. The school bus ahead blinked its caution while its contents emptied, backpack by backpack. He scanned the clusters of kids as they parted to start the short walk home. "Hey, I don't see our Mitch."

Cami had been admiring individual flowers in her bouquet but looked up with a jerk. "Well…where on earth could he be?" Her tone came riddled with surprise. "Did he say anything about an after-school activity when you took him to lunch earlier?"

The hair stood up on the back of Holt's neck as her words registered, and something sinister crept into his bliss-filled day. "Cami, I've been at Save Always all day." His leg twitched, ready to stomp the accelerator but the lanky bus lumbered through its turn-around up ahead. "Mr. Olson and I had lunch together in the deli. He likes to test the food on occasion. Why did you think that I had lunch with Mitch?"

She lowered the flowers several inches. "Because I got a call from Tammy in the school office saying Mitch's father was there, asking to take him to lunch. I asked for a name and when she stated yours, I gave her permission to authorize it."

Bile came up the back of his throat and he swallowed hard to knock it back. "Well, his father might have been there, but his name's not 'Holt.'" His voice sounded gravelly. He put his arm out to brace her shoulder as the situation reverberated through the car's interior. He felt her sob before he heard it and it ripped straight across his heart.

"Dear Lord, no," Cami uttered under her breath.

The school bus rumbled past and Holt floored the accelerator. "When we get home, you check everywhere. Mitch is a smart kid. He could have let himself in and be safe. Let's not think the worst until we know more."

"I want to call the school, as the office staff leaves at four and I need to talk to Tammy." The flowers started to quake as she lost control and a tiny pink petal floated to the floorboard.

"Don't let fear take over, or he wins." Holt ran his thumb across her whitened knuckles. When the car bounded up the driveway, he stomped the brakes and cut the ignition. Cami sprinted to the front door, unlocking it before he could even climb out. His eyes scanned the front yard. Nothing had been touched. The cat flinched from the bay window to meet Cami at the door, which he read as a signal that the boy hadn't come home yet. They would have to look inside anyway, before matters escalated.

Holt headed for the back patio. "Go change clothes after you search his room." He unlocked the sliding door and traced the stockade fence with a discerning look. No signs of the boy. He unlocked the back door to Joyce's half and flung himself inside, ripping his tie over his head and kicking off his dress shoes. The loss of time clamped a vice on his gut as he headed for the bedroom. There, a ratty T-shirt gave him a moment's solace as he grabbed it off the chair back. "God, please help us…and be with Mitch, wherever he is. Amen." He jumped into his shorts, slid on his sneakers in one fell swoop, and then out the door he ran.

~

Glued to the kitchen phone, Cami glanced around as the number rang for the school. She spotted Mitch's fourth grade picture on the refrigerator and made a mental note to snag it before they left. Holt came through the slider and locked it behind him as the call went through to the school office.

"Golden Valley Elementary, this is Tammy. How can I help you?"

"Hey Tammy, this is Cami Walsh, Mitch's mother. We spoke earlier today about permission for him to go off campus for lunch. Mitch didn't get off the bus like usual this afternoon, so I was wondering if you could check the sign-in sheet for me?" A hand rubbed her back between her shoulder blades and she remembered to breathe.

"Okay, here's today's list," Tammy soon replied. A pause filled the line "Well, look at that. They never came back in, at least not through the office."

Cami's temples pulsed and threatened to cave in. "You're saying they never signed back in? Are you sure?" She glanced up at a note Holt hastily scribbled in front of her.

"No, Ms. Walsh. This record shows Mitchell being signed out at eleven fifty this morning with no return time indicated. Guess I got busy with paperwork and lost track."

Cami forced an inhaled breath before she asked the next question. "I have Holt Ellis here with me now. He is not the man that signed Mitch out, Tammy. Can you describe that individual for me?" A finger pressed her lips telling her to hold her peace and allow the secretary to fill in the blanks.

"Oh dear. Well, he was a tall man and not too old. I even remember thinking they looked alike, you know, favored one another. He was a polite man and flashed a broad smile when he came in. Yes, that's right. I even recall that he winked at me when I called the teacher's room to summon Mitchell."

Cami bent in half at the secretary's description. Her mouth went dry from the realization that her son was in harm's way, in the hands of a man that never wanted to be his father until the day it hurt the most. As she faded into the blur of panic mode, Holt's hand took the receiver.

"Tammy, this is Holt Ellis. We're going to call the police next and have them meet us at your office. Could you stay there until we arrive? It'll only be five minutes at the most."

Cami forced her feet to move toward the refrigerator, where a well-posed picture of Mitch hung from a magnet-set clothespin. A firedog's image was glued to the clothespin, which had been carefully colored by the boy last year. The dog's message was to dial 9-1-1 in the event of an emergency. She choked on the realization that the emergency had now arrived.

As Holt led her toward the door, her steps felt choppy. She wondered if her legs knew how to outrun the dark fear that now chased her. She pinched Mitch's picture in her fingers and started to pull the door closed when another picture came to mind. She tore away from Holt's grasp and fled into her room, rummaging among her stacks of records. The clinic's folded brochure emerged and she snatched it from the pile. Today certainly represented no grand opening, but it might be a fitting end.

~

Holt angled toward the blue-flashing squad car. "Officer Gaines, good of you to answer our call." Cami ran past him and flew into the double doors of the school's front entrance.

The seasoned patrolman tucked a metal clipboard into the bend of his elbow."What time did the boy go missing?"

"Eleven-fifty, according to the school's sign-out sheet." Holt wished he could shorten both the time lag and the distance between him and the school. Sensing his urgency, the officer strode toward the building. Holt matched his gait and tried to read the police form.

"Do you have any idea of who might have wanted to check the boy out?"

"Yes, sir. I'm afraid we do. His name is Bo Ballard. He was a doctor at Golden Medical Center until Monday. His flirtatious behavior on duty got him in trouble and the director placed him on administrative leave yesterday. I believe the board of directors will be filing legal action against him by week's end."

"I see." Officer Gaines attempted to scribble the flow of information onto his report form as space allowed. "Anything else?"

"Well, I was waiting to pick up Miss Walsh after her shift Monday at three and Doctor Ballard came screeching through the back parking lot and threw a beer bottle at an SUV which shattered the windshield. That vehicle belonged to the center's director who had just relieved him of duty. I even have photos of the suspect in his BMW to prove it happened the way I'm telling you."

"I seem to recall that we got a vandalism claim about the clinic yesterday. How do you know the suspect was drinking? A lot of things are made of glass."

"This guy's selective. Seems he only drinks imported beer. I caught a glimpse of the label. And the glass was amber. Some of it still sits in a pile back in the lot." Holt bit his lip trying to filter out the negative dispersions that would help him characterize Bo Ballard. For Cami's sake he would keep the testimony clean of his own personal judgment, but heaven help him if he ever got the chance to finish off what he started the day Bo busted his lip. Holt pushed the door open and discovered a pasty-faced middle-aged woman standing behind the front counter.

"I'm Tammy Carlson, the school secretary. I'm the one who gave our Mitch away to a stranger."

Since she appeared on the verge of tears, Holt sensed the need to intervene and offer the woman a ray of hope. "Miss Carlson, I'm Holt Ellis. Please don't feel badly that you let Mitch go. You called Cami and she gave you her permission, as per the school's protocol. And this man isn't a stranger—in fact, he *is* Mitch's father." The officer looked up in sharp surprise as the secretary's mouth dropped open. Cami appeared at the far end of the hall dragging the missing boy's backpack. The sight prompted Holt to hurry. "He's the boy's biological father but nothing more. And that paternity, Officer Gaines, is part of the clinic's legal case pending against Doctor Ballard."

The officer pushed his pen, scribbling at record speed. "It looks like we've opened a real can of worms here. I'll need the boy's photo from the school records, ma'am."

"His mother brought one, just ask Cami for it." Holt held the office door open for her as she rapidly approached. "You have the photo, right? Officer Gaines is asking for one." He took the picture she produced and handed it over. In seconds, it transitioned from keepsake to part of the missing child report. His heart ached for Cami, and he placed a supportive hand on her back.

She glanced up at him, her gold-rimmed brown eyes brimming with tears. "I found his backpack still in his locker." Her voice quaked with restrained emotion.

"Which shows us the two weren't in cahoots." The officer jotted the detail into his report.

Holt sensed the situation had entered volatile territory, but thought he knew the boy better than to believe he'd be so gullible. "Mitchell knows about stranger danger, Officer Gaines. He only went with the guy because he regarded Bo as a family friend. Mitch didn't know anything about the legal case the clinic is mounting or that Bo had been placed on administrative leave."

"What about the paternity status? Did he know anything about that?" Officer Gaines poised his pen for the answer.

Holt clenched his teeth, not sure how Cami would deal with it.

"It was my choice to protect his innocent boyhood and shield him from the details." Cami confessed her approach with the blatant truth. A tear leaked over the rim but she ignored it with heroic restraint. "I asked him to wave a magic wand and help me catch a bad guy, so he was willing to be swabbed for the DNA sample. Doctor Harrison, the clinic's director, has the results and is protecting them as part of the legal case."

"Is this man, Bo Ballard, the boy's biological father, ma'am?" the officer asked.

Cami glanced up at Holt as the second tear found a route to mirror the first. A jagged breath escaped her frame. "Yes, Bo Ballard is Mitchell Walsh's biological father. He refused any claim further than that, and the conception occurred under duress, hence the legal case. He has no custody rights to Mitch and did not have my permission to take the boy from the safe haven of his school today."

The secretary clasped her hands to keep from wringing them. "But you did authorize his release."

Holt pressed his hip against Cami and looked Officer Gaines in the eye. "No. Cami gave *me* permission to take the boy. She released him to Holt Ellis, not Bo Ballard. The doctor used my name and misrepresented himself to get to the boy, knowing Cami would never let him have Mitch." He held the back of Cami's neck hoping to calm her down, but the forces of revelation were working against him as the whole thing came to a combustive head.

"May I see that sign-out sheet, Miss Carlson?" The officer motioned for possession and, compliant but shaky, the secretary handed him the clipboard. "And now may I have you sign this missing child form at the bottom, Mr. Ellis, to have authentication of your signature on record?"

Holt readily took the pen and wrote his name with his usual flourish, striking the capital 'E' with a staff from the bottom up before launching into the double curves. He had often regarded that staff as the steady influence of God upon his character, an allusion that would be especially potent today. A glimpse at the sign-in record revealed a block print rendering that didn't resemble his signature in the least. The police officer gave a harrumph.

"That seals the pre-meditated nature of this abduction for me," he said. "I'm calling in the Amber Alert to headquarters and we'll go from there. Do we know where this Bo Ballard lives?"

Holt folded Cami to his chest as she had broken down at the word "abduction."

"He lives in an upscale condo community on Clear Creek, just above the trailer park," Cami said, in staccato between sobs.

Holt felt a surge of advantage swing his way, as he had friends in that part of town. For the first time since the bus lights blinked their warning, he sensed a ray of hope.

"That subdivision is called 'Pyrite Place' isn't it?" The officer fingered his radio.

"That sounds about right." Holt recognized a cheap imitation when he saw one. If Bo was anything, he was fool's gold.

~

Coming out from under the bridge's shadow, Cami found strength in Holt's plan to tip off the locals as the police ran through protocol to track down Bo. Lucy and Leroy had now been educated as to who the bad guy was and asked to keep a sharp lookout for Mitch in the vicinity of the bridge. Displaying a depth of resourcefulness, Holt had the food pickup from the grocery store already in her car and made the Tuesday distribution as they went, albeit not from a bicycle. Her copy of the clinic's grand opening flyer was getting overtime use as she flashed the cover picture to anyone who would look.

Climbing up the bridge's arch, she could view a full section of the creek. She saw a scattering of people recreating in the crystal waters as the afternoon temperatures peaked. Activity on the museum's back deck drew her attention, as Miss Lily, their recent tour guide, led another group outdoors for part of her spiel. Momentarily ashamed at having to air her predicament, Cami swallowed her pride and ran down the bridge toward the civic center of town. After all, a little boy urgently needed help from his community. What could be shameful about that?

Chapter 22

Cami approached, breathless but persistent, as the group attempted to return indoors. "Miss Lily, please wait. Mitch, the little boy that played 'Fur Elise' last week on the orange piano, has been abducted from school today. The Golden police are leading the search, but I'm trying to get the word out about him as much as I can."

"Yes, I remember Mitch. Why, you're his mother, aren't you?" the guide asked.

"That's right, thank you so much for remembering." Cami extended the brochure. "Here's the suspect that might have Mitch. All I'm asking is that you contact the police if you should see them together. Mitch doesn't know that he's in danger so we have to act quickly. Please keep a lookout for the two of them." The photo made its way around the tour group and back to her.

The elderly woman's eyes softened as she placed a vein-knotted hand on her arm. "Rest assured, we will. I'll dismiss this group right away. Then you'll have that many more eyes out there looking for him, dearie."

"Bless you all for helping." Cami stepped down from the deck to continue along the creek run. She glanced between buildings and saw her car go by with Holt hanging out the window.

"Meet up at the trailer park," he shouted through cupped hands.

She raised the brochure, waved it in acknowledgment, and locked her sights on the next group recreating along the bank. Maybe they wouldn't mind their fun interrupted by a frantic mother, just this once.

~

Holt exited the car and found his friends under the picnic table awning as usual. He held the extra picture of Mitch that Cami had removed from her wallet and tucked it into his shirt pocket, freeing his hands for the food delivery. Big Tom waved from the table and Donnie made his move on the game board.

"Hey fellas. I've got something red hot and I need your help." Holt stepped toward them with the grocery bags. "The boy helping me with the food distribution, Mitch, was taken from school earlier today. The police are searching the culprit's condo up the creek from here but I'm trying to get the word out so we can help them. This guy Bo is wily."

Tom rubbed a hesitant hand over his beard stubble. "Thanks for bringing the food out anyway, Bicycle Man. You didn't have to go to all that trouble today— all things considered."

Holt tried to relax his diaphragm, but even the creek's gurgle didn't seem to help. "Well, the boy had big plans to make the loop himself this afternoon. I was already at the store this morning for a job interview, so I did the pickup part for him." He sat the food on the table.

Donnie busied his hands by putting away the game."How'd the interview work out?" He pinched his face up as though anticipating more bad news.

Holt produced the boy's picture and handed it off to Tom, who studied it a long moment. Tom handed it to Donnie as Holt turned and studied the water flow. A short blast of a police siren echoed down the mountainside and then jerked off as quickly as it started. "I landed the job, a real break for me, but it seems a moot point at the moment with the boy in peril and me standing here flat-footed."

"Doing everything humanly possible," Cami added as she arrived under the pavilion. "We're calling on all our friends for help with this one." She captured Holt's hand in hers.

An inexpressible relief washed over him as they connected, fighting the chaos and turmoil Bo had launched against them. Maybe this was what being a couple meant. The creek piqued his interest once again. The police siren clipped on once more and Donnie protected his ears, but not before his eyes went wild.

"Something's gone wrong." Holt turned upslope toward the noise. Shouts hailed above the siren, erratic at first, and then a constant barrage. The homeless men moved side-by-side as if to face the cataclysm together and Cami's hands started to tremble. Out of the corner of his eye, he spotted movement along the water. An ice pick jabbed his last intact nerve. A red kayak appeared, its pilot attacking the water by paddling full-tilt without regard for the rapids up ahead. Behind it, a poly line towed an inner tube filled with a wide-eyed, chunky boy.

"Mitchell!" Cami screamed, her voice shrill.

On instinct, Holt ran for the water's edge. When he turned to shout some directions back to her, Holt spied his two homeless friends fleeing in the opposite direction. The anger inside his chest left little room for disappointment at their abandonment.

"Head downstream." He waved with his hands, motioning down the path next to the rock-lined creek. To his relief, Cami broke off and ran like a gazelle, outdistancing the kayak, which still had to make the turn in the creek. Holt remembered seeing that stretch from their last visit to the homeless, a nasty set of boulders with rushing water between them. He slowed to better calibrate his footing as the kayaker turned his way. Recognition lit the man's face and he flashed an evil grin.

Blood boiling, Holt spat to clear his throat and braced himself for the upcoming icy plunge. "I'll kill you, Bo Ballard, so help me. If anything happens to the boy, I'll kill you myself." The threat burned across his vocal chords, leaving him hoarse. To his utter amazement, the paddler threw up his end of the poly line in response and set the tube free. Just as the water sucked into a V between the rocks, the kayaker manipulated the boat into proper position and glided through the gap without incident. In an instant, Holt realized the tube would not fare as well. When Mitchell locked gazes with him, it left him only one focus—the boy—which meant the kidnapper would get away scot free.

Mitch lost his grip and slid inside the ring. "Holt—help me!"

Holt took three rocky steps toward the bend and assessed the foaming rapids one last time. "Lean back and hold on," he yelled.

The front of the inner tube dipped and slid between the rocks cooperatively as the waves frothed and the water churned. Approaching the cascade of the lower falls, the tube promptly inverted. All Holt could see was one chunky leg until even that slid beneath the surface. He read the wipeout as his invitation to hit the water, and dove into the glassy pool below the run. As his hands pushed off the rocky bottom, the coldness of the ice melt waters collapsed his lungs like some punishment for inviting himself along. He had entered a dark, churned-up world.

~

Cami tried to yell but the words wouldn't form through her heavy panting. With a glance over her shoulder, she could see the red kayak bearing down on midstream, a section currently spattered with innocent thrill seekers. She needed to warn them, these same people that she had spoken peacefully to only minutes ago, that this was the devil incarnate who had taken her son—her beloved son that she had spent the last eight years of her life nurturing. Evil rode the current in a boat of red, and she needed their help to stop it.

The first set of rocky steps down to the creek loomed beyond a large cottonwood tree. A sturdy group of college guys from the nearby mining school had been sunning on the flat rock island and would be more than enough manpower, if she could warn them in time.

"Hey guys. Help me now. The kidnapper is coming." She waved the brochure at the group on the rocks.

Bo paddled with intrepid skill, his plan becoming evident with each stroke. Water swept by the rock island on both sides, and he would pass through the top section just beyond the reach of the young men. "There in the red kayak—stop him," she screamed, her tone escalating. Three young men clambered up on the rock and courageously dove into the water, but missed the slender boat. Turning to navigate the next set of rapids, the kayaker laughed like a maniac.

Cami felt her blood go as cold as the creek. Without thinking, she began running downstream again. "God, help me get him." She inhaled and assessed the stretch up ahead. "No getting away." The words seethed through her teeth, seeming distinct from the prayer. Or were they?

~

Holt surfaced and sucked a breath to appease his demanding lungs. The inner tube had caught in an eddy pool, now boy-less. It spun senselessly among the tall reeds. He guessed the creek bed to be over ten feet deep, as the spot cradled the bend and had been carved out by flushing currents for eons. The water's surface remained unbroken, with no visible sign of the missing boy.

Holt mentally divided the area into quadrants and took a breath to get started on the first swim-through. The downstream quad would be first, and it appeared darkly uncooperative. He thrashed his hands as he propelled himself below the surface, kicked deeper, and then pushed back up against the rocky bottom. This time when he surfaced, he came up right beside the tube. He pulled a breath and thought his ears were ringing until he realized police cars were approaching the water park with sirens blaring.

He shoved the tube aside, exhaled, and took a final breath before plunging below again. This time, he found a shoe and grabbed it like insurance that he'd be able to finish the job with some success. Something silver flashed up ahead, but he found only a school of minnows lurking in the depths. He trailed his bubbles up to the surface where his lungs exploded for air. He slung the shoe toward the sidewalk as a police car approached the rec area parking lot. Halfway done with the reconnaissance, he still had no boy. Time had shifted sides of the raft.

~

The creek narrowed along its next stretch, and Cami determined to use that in her favor. More revelers swam near the next access steps and some of them had boogey boards for their water play. They could use them against the kayaker—if she could get it set up in time. She looked behind her and Bo was plying his shoulder power with the current to hit maximum escape speed.

"It's him—the kidnapper!" She shouted a warning as she ran toward the steps. "Help me form a blockade to stop him." A couple of tanned guys pulled their boards out of the rapids and moved upriver to post some interference. Cami came down into the water for the first time, the flow sliding past her legs as she grappled for a handhold along the bank. A child handed her a junior-sized board. She waded out toward the others and braced for the kayak's approach. Bo paddled harder. Her partners decided to work from each side and allow their boards to take the brunt of the kayak's bow, front-and-center.

"Move back!" Bo lunged forward, stabbed his paddle into the water, and began to ram the makeshift blockade.

While the other volunteers frightened away from the madman, Cami didn't flinch. Bo must have seen her stand firm because he stretched for a bow reach and buried his paddle right into her midsection. Reflexively, she turned her hip into the blow, grabbed at her target and pulled back, which gained her the paddle but not the boater.

The next set of rapids sucked the torpedo-shaped craft into its influence but now there was little Bo could do to rectify his position. He spun around and went down the falls backward and the kayak rolled completely over. Beyond the foam, the craft righted and the passenger came up with a war cry, his long arms emulating his paddle.

Cami forced her feet back onto the bank, and this time found reinforcements in uniform waiting on the steps.

"Get the medic, she's bleeding," Officer Gaines signaled in haste. He gave her a hand out of the water.

Cami glanced down and the left side of her shirt dripped blood as red as the kayak through a tear in the fabric. "No. I have him on the run now." She broke out of the officer's well-meaning grasp. Refortified, she brandished the paddle as she ran downriver to the next set of steps, putting her right behind the Pioneer Museum. This episode was history-in-the-making all right, and she was determined to come out on top when the story had occasion to be retold.

~

Something about the water seemed different through here, and Holt felt unfamiliar warmth flush his skin. Out of breath, he forced himself to stay down. His mind cleared, and a silent glint of light penetrated the water column. He sensed peace underwater, as if God was with him in the Spirit, and the pressure on his lungs evaporated at the thought. He kicked like a dolphin to propel himself forward, where something bulky curled in the water. As he approached, he recognized the limp boy, floating face down. Hooking a hand in his shorts, he hauled Mitch to the surface, half elated and half scared to death.

When he broke the surface, two officers and an EMT waited on the bank. The officers waded into the shallows to drag him in. Mitch's unresponsive bulk left his hands while he attempted to refill his burning lungs. As he knelt on the rocks, Holt watched them move the boy's body toward the ambulance. There, a man began to administer CPR, which sickened Holt to watch. A retching sound led the EMT to turn the boy on his side. Soon, his small frame flexed into a coil. As the man coaxed him through a return to consciousness, Holt regained circulation in his legs.

Invigorated, Holt looked downstream. A mass of people congregated along the lower bank. He pulled himself to his feet and ran toward them.

~

"Help me, Lily!" Cami spotted the older woman above her on the museum deck. Unable to wait, she charged down the wet steps as the errant kayak twisted against the creek's flow and bobbed like a cork. The smile on the kayaker's face had disappeared, as gone as his paddle. She had the upper hand now, and better traction than a floating piece of tapered fiberglass. Taking time to place her feet solidly between the rocks, Cami waded out to catch her prey.

A commotion back on the bank caught her attention. Lily had arrived with an antiquated length of mule harness with which Officer Gaines provided assistance. Between the hardy leather straps, a fine mesh of tatted string interlaced, meant for keeping the flies off the mules' backs as they toiled. Together, the rescuers fed it down the bank toward Cami's position midstream. She hesitated to release the paddle to claim the front edge of the snare net with both hands, but then a man rushed into the water behind the hefty officer and yanked the paddle from her hands as the kayak came within spitting distance.

Holt shook water from his hair and waded upstream like a man possessed. "I believe the next attempt is all mine. The EMTs have Mitch—he's going to be fine."

Cami gave Officer Gaines a panicked look and he signaled to his men downstream. Lily stood braced for action, her thin arms taut with the leather line. Cami took a section of harness and twisted it in her grip.

"Let him go first," the officer directed, pulling back on the harness. "We'll stand ready."

Cami knew Bo better than anyone else, though. She promised to count to seven and wait no more. The kayak came at them, askew with the shoreline and ramrod swift. Holt took a swing with the paddle and Bo grabbed it with his arm's-length advantage. The paddle swing had been merely a decoy, as Holt landed a quick right-hand punch and a left slug soon followed. Defensive, Bo used the paddle to roll the kayak, and soon avoided Holt's reach underwater. Holt dropped into the swift current out of sight.

Prompted into action, Cami pulled the leading edge of the harness and waded out. Another set of rapids fell below her station and she knew Bo wouldn't go down them capsized, so she waited him out. The netting pulled taut as Officer Gaines positioned himself slightly upstream. The kayak soon leveled with the flow as it entered their snare blind. The third point of triangulation, Lily held her place in the shallows, giving them enough line to make the trap work.

Almost on cue, the kayak righted in front of Cami. She threw the heaviest part of the harness and it splashed past the kayak's bow, netting the paddler. Caught across the rocks framing the rapids, the kayak careened as Bo struggled to get free.

Holt reappeared, and in a surge of power wrestled the paddle away, with a heavy-handed whack across the man's back. Officer Gaines rushed out to grab his prisoner when the net gave way with a wet snap. The kayak slipped down the rapids backward and took its operator with it.

Cami stared farther down at the bridge area, which was seething with full-strength uniformed reinforcements. An ambulance crossed above, lights flashing and sirens blaring. Her knees buckled beneath her at the thought of her son suffering. When she made dry land, she came up braced in Holt's arms, thoroughly waterlogged and operating on fumes. If only she had eaten something earlier. Growing faint, she noticed the homeless people huddled under the bridge.

~

As much as he wanted to cave in the skull of the escaping kayaker, Holt was not about to leave Cami's side again. Officer Gaines dodged past him and ran toward his troops on the far side of the bridge. Holt pulled Cami against him and locked an arm around her waist until she winced and protested from the pressure.

Looking closer, he saw blood covering half her body, and her face white as a sheet. He tried to get her off the concrete sidewalk so he could place her down in the grass. "You need medical help."

"No stopping. Not until we get Bo. Promise me." She pulled at his shirt until they were inches apart. Her gaze pierced his.

"This goes against my better judgment." He gave a shake of his head, savoring the struggle between head and heart, knowing they were about to come out on top together. The odds were stacked against the rogue doctor now. He could see all the help accumulating by the bridge. From this lowest crease between the mountains, they were gaining momentum in the fight against evil—only it didn't feel like victory yet. He stood and gave her a hand up, watching the backward boat approach its final destiny.

The kayak turned crosswise to the current, about to enter the late afternoon shadows under the bridge. Just beyond, Officer Gaines stood on the same rock where Holt had delivered countless food packs, his men poised for the takedown. Holt brought Cami up along the shade-lined bank to witness the downfall of a giant. When a slender arm appeared on Cami's far side, Holt leaned forward and was pleasantly surprised to see Lily join them, her eyes steely.

The final ensnarement for the boat was being set in a flurry of controlled commotion, but it wasn't the police trap that Holt had anticipated. Leroy stepped into the deepest channel, his long legs a marked advantage, with Big Tom and Donnie right beside him, both flexing their muscular arms. Even Lucy braved the water, along with several other nameless souls Holt had fed. Together they formed a human barrier that no boat could pass.

Unable to believe his eyes, Holt blinked several times as the bridge overshadowed the kayak. "What are they doing?" he muttered under his breath as he tucked her against him.

"Taking justice into their own hands," Cami replied, "a true act of bravery."

Exhausted, they watched the scene unfold. The boat collided with the homeless of Golden and they lifted it completely out of the water with Bo inside, suspended in their mighty collective grip. Lily motioned to a bystander who took a photo of the incredible scene. Leroy led the team toward the east bank where the police waited to manhandle Bo out of his escape craft and secure him into confinement. An intense feeling of closure swept over Holt as Cami leaned into him and then became dead weight in his arms.

"Sweet Lord above," Lily whispered. "Medic! We need a medic!" Her shrill call turned heads all the way to the bridge.

Holt laid Cami in the grass with tenderness as the EMTs raced across the sidewalk, their gear belts clicking on approach. On his knees at her side, Holt's heart squeezed in anguish inside his heaving chest. He brushed her hair off her face. A gurney landed beside her. With a sudden lift, the medical team had Cami ready for transport.

"Ride with us," the trailing EMT said, more like a question than a command. Lily helped Holt to his feet and they followed the rescuers up the grassy bank.

Headed for the ambulance, Holt noticed that both of his shins were cut and bleeding, a familiar trait that seemed to mark his route to salvation. With mountain-melt water clinging to his skin, Holt realized what a moveable feast it was to be alive. He tossed a wave to Lily through the closing doors of the ambulance, a final farewell to history. If this is what it felt like to love someone, he was going to need saving a lot more often.

Cami groaned and twisted toward him on the gurney. "So hungry."

"I've got some tiny donuts," the EMT offered. The vehicle lurched forward up the embankment.

"Yeah, she'd love some of those." Holt bent closer, locked one hand on the gurney's rail and stroked her jaw line in admiration. She rewarded him with a weak smile. An open-ended pack of chocolate-dipped donuts appeared between them. "How about a lifeline?" he asked with a tease.

"Oh, so now you're saving me?" she asked. A donut found its way between her lips and the rest of her comment became muffled.

"Turnabout *is* fair play," he whispered, holding the next lucky morsel above her mouth. A smile twitched and lured him down into her zone where their lips met, a sweet connection for an ambulance ride built for two.

Epilogue

Cami yelped in delight and picked her feet up off the back pedals as Holt steered the tandem bike down the east flank of the bridge. He navigated the terrain and braked beside the flat rock where Mitchell stood with the food offering for the homeless. Ever the protective mother, Cami turned to search for their friends, but no one wandered out from under the structure.

"Wonder where everyone is today?" She scratched a circular pattern onto Holt's back with her nails. He arched like a cat for a few moments, and then turned and pointed atop the bridge. Leroy waved his long arms like a flagman on the bow of a ship, which made her smile.

Holt swung his leg over the bike seat and motioned to Mitch. "Come on. Let's go see what they're up to."

The boy scrambled off the rock and ran up the

bridge flank to join the others. Tom and Donnie flanked Lucy, a proud new resident of the trailer park. Leroy soon joined them. Everyone seemed to be congregating on the span that crossed Clear Creek. Holt locked her arm in his as they ventured up the slope.

Cami took an exaggerated breath while she paused to enjoy the view. The sun had lowered in the dusky blue sky and the creek's rushing waters looked like liquid gold as she admired the surroundings. What a day this was—a day unlike any other. Her foot landed on the bridge's pavement and Holt pulled her single file in front of him to make the crossing.

"Hey, look at all this food." She nodded toward several old-timey pushcarts laden with delightful finger food. "There must be some kind of street celebration going on. And there's Lily from the museum, and Officer Gaines, too. All our friends are here—how fun."

Holt poked her side, but held his peace as they arrived at the top of the arch. Lily greeted her with a hug and Leroy tipped his hat toward them both. Lucy shuffled over and produced a tiny nosegay of delicate wildflowers, offering them to Cami with a gap-toothed smile.

Somewhere a violin started playing a soft refrain. She wrinkled her nose in a coy smile until the song registered. Her brow knit, she glanced around trying to read the looks on people's faces. Everyone seemed to be equally transported as the violin carried into the next stanza.

"That's 'Fur Elise,' Mitch's song," she whispered as she glanced over at her son. The boy looked like he was about to burst with some secret, but bit his lips together and stood quietly. Cami sensed being held in a safe place here on the bridge among so many friends. The realization left her lighthearted.

"And now we're making it our song." Holt took her hand and gave it a kiss. Lily stepped closer and passed him a little velvet box, which he took with a grin. He turned to Cami, offered her a double dimpled smile and allowed a few seconds to pass, obviously enjoying the moment. Holt then dropped to one knee, but didn't take his eyes from hers.

Cami gasped. The nosegay followed her hands up to her mouth as it dawned on her what kind of street party was actually transpiring—the engagement kind. Though she'd hoped this day might come, she never guessed how transcendent it would feel with Holt leading it.

"Camille Walsh, now that you have saved me from myself, would you please marry me and share a life each glorious day that God might give us together?" He waited for her response.

Myriad feelings raced in her chest. She pressed the nosegay against her throbbing heart. Seconds ticked by as she closed and opened her eyes, looking down at the man who had outlasted his scrapes and scars to win her affections and fill her life with love.

"Why, Holt Ellis," she replied. "I cannot imagine riding through life with anyone else but Bicycle Man. My answer is yes, I will marry you."

He wiggled a glitter-chunked ring onto her finger and she held it up to a spattering of approving applause. The diamond caught the sun's rays and shimmered them back onto the earth, lending a fitting tribute to the close of day. The creek gurgled beneath them in response, its valley holding the brooding mountains back in the distance where they belonged.

The End

ABOUT THE AUTHOR

Cindy M. Amos writes contemporary and historical inspirational fiction in natural settings to combine her background in field ecology with her Christian walk of faith. Her books weave nature's intricate beauty with humanity's spiritual relevance into seamless plot-driven romance stories with up-lifting, God-honoring endings. A full-time freelance writer with numerous national magazine publications, Ms. Amos has placed as a finalist in the American Christian Fiction Writers' Genesis and Mid-America Romance Authors' Fiction from the Heartland contests. She serves as the south central Kansas chapter secretary for ACFW and writes from Wichita, Kansas where she shares a home with her aviation industry husband and two come-and-go college-aged sons. With the expanse of the tallgrass prairie hers to wander, she loves to name the wildflowers in bloom and has a fondness for the badger on the pond dam.

~Envir-Romance… where love lingers on the landscape~

OTHER BOOKS BY CINDY M. AMOS

LANDSCAPES OF MERCY SERIES

Book One   *Redeeming River Rancher*